彩圖實境

旅遊英語

會話模擬練功

P. Walsh / Peichien Sun /
Feiyueh Chang 著

Traveling
With English

目錄

學英語最怕憑空想像。讀者一定有過這種經驗：空有一堆字彙，真正到了國外，畫面卻與字彙搭不起來，依然什麼都看不懂，什麼都説不出口。的確，「百聞不如一見」這句話不是沒有道理的。

本書創新採用**大量實景照片**來介紹字彙，以視覺輔助記憶，不僅學來輕鬆，印象也特別深刻，不容易遺忘。

全書 17 個章節，**涵蓋機場、交通、住宿、購物等重要主題**，依照一般旅遊行程排列，貼近實際使用習慣。不論跟團、自助旅行，本書都是您不可或缺的好幫手。

Part 1 Key Terms

彩色圖解字彙

用「看」的學單字，絕對比憑空死背有效。本書以大量的彩色照片，具體呈現單字所代表的意義，豐富你的視覺，減輕學習壓力。

PART 1 Key Terms

❶ airport 機場
❷ check-in counter 登機櫃檯
❸ e-ticket 電子機票
❹ passport 護照
❺ visa 簽證

延伸字彙片語

意義較為抽象、不適合用圖片説明的單字與片語，收錄在「彩色圖解字彙」後，不遺漏任何重要字彙。

㉑ carry-on luggage/bag 隨身行李
㉒ city map 市區地圖
㉓ book a ticket / make a reservation 訂機票
㉔ flight number 航班編號
㉕ check in 辦理登記手續
㉖ one-way ticket (US) 單程票 (美國)
㉗ round-trip ticket (US) 來回票 (美國)
㉘ single ticket (UK) 單程票 (英國)
㉙ return ticket (UK) 來回票 (英國)
㉚ open return (ticket) 回程時間不定 (機票)
㉛ direct/nonstop flight 直飛班機
㉜ connecting flight 轉接班機
㉝ red-eye flight 紅眼航班；夜間航班
㉞ reconfirm the ticket 再確認機位
㉟ excess baggage 超重行李
㊱ baggage allowance 行李限額
㊲ baggage claim tag 行李提領證
㊳ departure 起飛
㊴ local time 當地時間
㊵ on time 準時
㊶ delay 誤點
㊷ cancel 取消
㊸ tourist information 旅遊資訊

Part 2 Conversations

會話練習

本書 17 個單元，每單元皆有 2 到 3 則會話練習，讀者可藉由簡單的會話練習，學習英語的實際運用。

PART 2 • Conversations

01 Making a Reservation 訂機票

Raymond	I'd like to make a reservation to Los Angeles for next Monday.
Ground Staff	Just a second and I'll check the schedule.
Raymond	I'll need an economy ticket with an open return.
Ground Staff	American Airlines has a flight leaving at 9:25 a.m.
Raymond	I guess that's OK. What time should I check in?
Ground Staff	You have to be there two hours before departure time.

| 雷蒙 | 我要預訂下禮拜一去洛杉磯的機票。 |
| 地勤人員 | 請稍等，我查一下時刻表。 |

Part 3 Pattern Drills

PART 3 • Pattern Drills

01 I'd like to check in.
我要辦住宿登記。（已預約住宿）

Reception	Good afternoon. May I help you?
Steve	Yes. I made a reservation and I'd like to check in.
Reception	Your name, p
Steve	Steve Johnso
Reception	Oh, yes. A d
Steve	Yes, it is.
Reception	Would you pl

1
May I have your name, please?
[Your name]
A triple room for one night.
Yes, I will.

2
Could you spell out your name?
C-H-A-N-G
A suite for three nights.
Certainly.

會話實境模擬練習

根據會話編寫出各種模擬實境，包含**各種情境可替換的詞彙或常用句**，反覆透過會話架構的模擬實境練習，讓你出國免緊張，情境一出現，自然溝通零障礙！

提供替換用語

以色彩標示對應之**替換用語**，方便對照練習，一目瞭然。

補充旅遊資訊

依據場合需要，補充各種貼心的小資訊。

常見的機場標誌
Common Airport Signs

Information ?!
Information Counter 服務台

Departure
Departure Hall 出境大廳

Arrival

Gate 20 | Gate 21

Bag claim
Baggage hall

Lift

Check-in

Customs Control

At the Airport

Chapter

1

搭飛機旅行：
在機場

001

1 **airport** 機場

2 **check-in counter** 登機櫃檯

3 **e-ticket** 電子機票

4 **passport** 護照

5 **visa** 簽證

6 **boarding pass** 登機證

7 **luggage cart/trolley** 行李推車

⑧ **airline** 航空公司

⑨ **scale** 磅秤

⑩ **morning flight** 早班飛機

⑪ **night flight** 晚班飛機

⑫ **departure board**
起飛時刻表

⑬ **security gate** 安全門

⑭ **moving walkway**
電動步道

⑮ duty free shop 免稅商店

⑯ (departure) gate 登機門

⑰ departure lounge 候機室

⑱ runway 跑道

⑲ **fragile item** 易碎物品　⑳ **VIP lounge** 機場貴賓室

㉑ **carry-on luggage/bag**
隨身行李

㉒ **city map** 市區地圖

㉓ **book a ticket /
make a reservation** 訂機票

㉔ **flight number** 航班編號

㉕ **check in** 辦理登記手續

㉖ **one-way ticket** (US) 單程票（美國）

㉗ **round-trip ticket** (US) 來回票（美國）

㉘ **single ticket** (UK) 單程票（英國）

㉙ **return ticket** (UK) 來回票（英國）

㉚ **open return (ticket)** 回程時間不定（機票）

㉛ **direct/nonstop flight** 直飛班機

㉜ **connecting flight** 轉接班機

㉝ **red-eye flight** 紅眼航班；夜間航班

㉞ **reconfirm the ticket** 再確認機位

㉟ **excess baggage** 超重行李

㊱ **baggage allowance** 行李限額

㊲ **baggage claim tag** 行李提領證

㊳ **departure** 起飛

㊴ **local time** 當地時間

㊵ **on time** 準時

㊶ **delay** 誤點

㊷ **cancel** 取消

㊸ **tourist information** 旅遊資訊

1 Making a Reservation 訂機票 005

Raymond	I'd like to make a reservation to Los Angeles for next Monday.
Ground Staff	Just a second and I'll check the schedule.
Raymond	I'll need an economy ticket with an open return.
Ground Staff	American Airlines has a flight leaving at 9:25 a.m.
Raymond	I guess that's OK. What time should I check in?
Ground Staff	You have to be there two hours before departure time.

雷蒙	我要預訂一張下禮拜一去洛杉磯的機票。
地勤人員	請稍等，我查一下時刻表。
雷蒙	我要經濟艙，回程時間不定的來回票。
地勤人員	美國航空公司有一架班機，在早上 9 點 25 分起飛。
雷蒙	這個可以，我應該什麼時候去辦理登機手續？
地勤人員	你要在飛機起飛前兩小時到達那裡。

American Airlines 美國航空

❷ Checking In 辦理登機手續 006

Raymond	I'd like to check in.
Ground Staff	May I have your ticket and passport, please?
Raymond	Here you are. I'd like a window seat.
Ground Staff	No problem. Put your baggage on the scale, please.
Raymond	All right.
Ground Staff	OK. Here's your ticket, boarding pass, passport and baggage claim tag. You'll be boarding at Gate 8. The boarding time is 9 a.m.
Raymond	Thank you very much.

雷蒙	我要辦理登機手續。
地勤人員	請給我您的機票和護照。
雷蒙	在這裡。我想要靠窗的座位。
地勤人員	沒問題。請把行李放在磅秤上。
雷蒙	好。
地勤人員	可以了。這是您的機票、登機證、護照和行李提領證。您的登機時間是早上9點，請由八號登機門登機。
雷蒙	非常謝謝你。

依民航局安檢新規定，超過100 c.c. 的液體不能放在手提行李內登機，瑞士刀、剪刀等物品亦禁止隨身攜帶登機。

因此在準備行李時，別忘了將化妝水、乳液、飲料等液體，以及瑞士刀、刀片等利器放進托運行李中，以免在通過安檢時被沒收或強制丟棄喔。

❶ Making a Reservation 訂機票

Raymond	I'd like to make a reservation to Los Angeles for next Monday.
Ground Staff	Just a second and I'll check the schedule.
Raymond	I'll need an economy ticket with an open return.
Ground Staff	American Airlines has a flight leaving at 9:25 a.m.
Raymond	I guess that's OK. What time should I check in?
Ground Staff	You have to be there two hours before departure time.

Subject: Conference.
Made flight, but guy next to me so unfriendly

1

for tomorrow
the computer
a business ticket
China Airlines
When am I supposed to check in?

2

for next month
for you
a round-trip ticket
EVA Air Airlines
How early do I need to arrive at the airport?

3

for the 7th of December
the seat opening
a one-way reservation
Cathay Pacific Airlines
When should I arrive at the airport?

Make up your own conversation.

❷ Checking In 辦理登機手續 〔008〕

Raymond   I'd like to check in.

Ground Staff May I have your ticket and passport, please?

Raymond   Here you are. I'd like a window seat.

Ground Staff No problem. Put your baggage on the scale, please.

Raymond   All right.

Ground Staff OK. Here's your ticket, boarding pass, passport, and
             baggage claim tag. You'll be boarding at Gate 8. The
             boarding time is 9 a.m.

Raymond   Thank you very much.

1

Would you give me

I'd like an aisle seat.

bags

departure time is 9:30 a.m.

2

Would you show me

A window seat, please.

luggage

departure time may be delayed by one hour

3

May I see

An aisle seat, please.

suitcases

boarding time will be announced

4

Make up your own conversation.

第一次出國時，難免緊張興奮，甚至會不知該如何是好。
別擔心，只要跟著以下的流程走，一切簡單輕鬆！

1 櫃檯劃位 check-in counter

機場有兩個不同的大廳，分別是**出境大廳**
（**Departure Hall**）及**入境大廳**（**Arrival
Hall**）。出國時一定要前往出境大廳，到
了那裡找到要搭乘的航空公司**劃位櫃檯**
（**check-in counter**），即可辦理手續。

check-in counter 報到櫃檯

有時不見得所有航空公司都有自己的劃位
櫃檯，但無櫃檯的航空公司一定會委託
另一家航空公司代為處理，這時只要看一
下標示即可找到正確的櫃檯。一般說來，
出國旅遊須在飛機起飛前兩個小時到達機
場，所辦理之手續如下：

→ 核對證件：**機票或電子機票（ticket /
e-ticket）、護照（passport）、簽證（visa）**

→ 託運行李：**過磅（weigh）**、檢查、
發行李牌。行李若**超重（overweight）**，
則須支付**行李超重費（overweight
charge; excess baggage charge）**。
每家航空公司對**託運行李（checked
baggage）**與**手提行李（carry-on
baggage / hand baggage）**限制的件數
與重量不盡相同，建議事先查好所搭乘
的航空公司規定，以免在託運時才發現
過重或超過件數。

weighing baggage 行李過磅

→ 選座位：各種座位的說法如下：

靠窗座位 window seat
走道座位 aisle seat
中間座位 middle seat

→ 領取登機證（boarding pass）：如果有
託運行李，行李牌則一併交回，或是直接
貼在機票上。登機證上會註明**班機號碼**
（**flight number**）、**登機門**（**boarding
gate**）、**座位號碼**（**seat number**），
有時也會寫上**登機時間**（**boarding
time**）。 如果你是某航空公司的會員，
或者已累積一定的哩程點數可以**升等**
（**upgrade**），可於此時告知航空公司，
請其查詢是否尚有機位可以升等。

boarding gate 登機門

另外，需依各機場的規定付**機場稅**（**airport
tax; departure tax**）。有些國家如中國大
陸及泰國等，不像國內的機場稅已於機票內
含，都需要另付機場稅，請於出發前確認，
否則到了當地機場時，身上沒有該國現金而
付不了機場稅，這樣可是非常麻煩的喔。

2 查驗護照 passport inspection

departure stamp 出境章

將護照及登機證交付查驗，護照也會蓋
上一個註明日期的**出境章**（**departure
stamp**），表示已經出國囉！有時會問
一兩個簡單的問題，如為何停留該國、
接下來要去哪國之類的問題。

現在各國的國際機場也設置了**自動查驗
通關系統**（**e-Gate**），只要事先完成自
動通關申辦，以後在出入境時就能省去
排隊的時間，加快通關速度。

e-Gate 自動查驗通關系統

台灣申辦自動查驗通關辦法：

■ 申辦資格：
1. 年滿 **14** 歲、身高 **140cm** 以上。
2. 未受禁止出國處分之有戶籍國民。

■ 申辦文件：護照、身分證（或駕照、健保卡）／居留證。

■ 申辦地點：機場、移民署服務站、外交部領事事務局（詳細地點請上網查閱）。

metal detector 金屬探測器

❸ 安全檢查 security inspection

在這裡又分為人走的「**金屬探測器**」（metal detector），及隨身行李和物品走的「**行李 X 光**」（baggage X-ray）兩項檢查裝置。

baggage X-ray 行李X光

❹ 進入登機門 boarding gate

憑著登機證找到正確的登機門，之後便可以在**候機室**（lounge）等候登機囉！這時如果時間充裕，還可以到**免稅商店**（duty free shop，簡稱 DFS）逛逛。

切記！在免稅店買東西，一定要出示護照跟登機證才能購買喔！若是需要回國再提領，可以在提貨後向現場服務人員洽詢**寄物服務**（baggage storage service）。

lounge 候機室

❺ 登機 boarding

到了登機時間時，航空公司會開始廣播請大家登機；通常都是**商務艙**（business class）的旅客先登機，之後是老人或是有小孩的旅客，接著是**經濟艙**（economy class）的旅客按照機位前後，從後半段的乘客先登機。

duty free shop (DFS) 免稅商店

出境攜帶物品限制
Baggage Policy & Restrictions

託運行李禁止品項
What NOT to pack in your checked baggage

■ **行動電源（power bank）、鋰電池（lithium battery）／含有鋰電池的電子產品**：須放置隨身行李，因鋰電池在溫度與壓力變化劇烈的情況下，有膨脹甚至是起火爆炸的風險。

■ **打火機（lighter）**：須隨身攜帶，且每人限帶一個傳統型打火機。

■ **高壓式噴瓶（high pressure sprayer bottle）**：有些噴霧為高壓式噴瓶（如髮膠），在行李艙有爆炸的危險。

隨身行李禁止品項
What NOT to pack in your carry-on baggage

■ **各式刀剪類或尖銳物品**：各種刀剪，如剪刀、美工刀、修眉刀、指甲剪等；或是如開罐器、圓規等鋒利物品，一律禁止攜帶上機。

■ **超過 100 毫升的液體**：不得攜帶超過 100 毫升（100 c.c.）的液體上機（註：安全考量，因任何不超過 100 毫升的液體危害性極小），且所有裝有液體、膠狀或噴霧類的瓶罐須裝在不超過一公升（1000 c.c.）的可重複密封之透明夾鏈袋中。

■ **收合後超過 60 公分的自拍桿（selfie stick）／超過 60 公分的腳架（tripod）**：管徑超過 1 公分、且長度超過 60 公分的自拍桿或腳架，因具有攻擊性也禁止攜帶上機。

線上訂機票
**Booking Flight
Tickets Online**

SEARCH NOW! CHEAP FLIGHTS
Fast. Booking. Top Offers.

ONE WEEK ONLY: GLOBAL DEALS ON SPRING TRAVEL

EXPLORE OUR OFFERS

Journey Airline

① LEAVING FROM
From (ie. NYC)

② GOING TO
To (ie. LON)

③ DEPARTING ON
4-03-2018

④ RETURNING ON
7-03-2018

⑤ ADULTS
2

CLASS
Economy

⑥

⑦ One way

⑧ Round trip

⑨ Multi-city

SEARCH FLIGHTS

MESSAGE   LEARN MORE ⚙-

❶ Leaving From 出發地
❷ Going To 目的地
❸ Departure Date 出發日期
❹ Return Date 回程日期
❺ Passenger Details 旅客資料

❻ Class 艙等
❼ One Way 單程行程
❽ Round Trip 來回行程
❾ Multi-City 多航點行程

To	Olin@smail.com
Subject	Your booking confirmation 預訂確認

Hi Olivia, **❿**

We've attached your travel itinerary which has details of your flights, add-ons, and payment.

Remember to print a copy of the travel itinerary for your trip.

You can make changes to your booking up to 24 hours before departure. Just click on "Manage Your Booking" below to make changes.

Thanks for choosing Journey Airline.

Journey Airline

⓫
Booking Ref.
M5XAAB

奧莉薇亞，您好：

隨信已附上您的行程資訊，包含了班機、附加項目以及付款細節等資料。
請記得在出發前影印一份行程資訊副本。
您最遲可在出發前 24 小時前修改您的預訂項目，只要點擊以下的「管理預訂」即可更改。
感謝您搭乘旅程航空。

旅程航空 敬上

❿ Booking Confirmation Email 預訂確認信
⓫ Booking Reference Number 訂位代碼

電子機票 1
E-ticket

Airlines

YOUR TICKET-ITINERARY

YOUR BOOKING NUMBER : **WXIKXI** ①

Flight ②	From ③	⑦	To		Aircraft ④	Class/Status ⑤ ⑥
WK 2200	Montreal-Trudeau (YUL) Thu May-04-2019	17:15	Frankfurt (FRA) Fri May-05-2019	06:30+1	333	Y Confirmed
WK 2495	Frankfurt (FRA) T1 Fri May-05-2019	07:50	Amsterdam (AMS) Fri May-05-2019	09:00	321	Y Confirmed
WK 2293	Munich (MUC) T2 Mon May-22-2019	15:30	Montreal-Trudeau (YUL) 17:50 Mon May-22-2019		340	Y Confirmed

Passenger Name ⑧	Ticket Number ⑨	Frequent Flyer Number ⑩	Special Needs ⑪
(1) JONES, JOHN/MR.	012-3456-789012	000-123-456	Meal: VGML

Purchase Description ⑫	Price ⑬	
Fare (LLXSOAR, LLXGSOAR)	CAD	558.00
Canada - Airport Improvement Fee		15.00
Canada - Security Duty		17.00
Canada - GST #1234-5678		1.05
Canada - QST #12345-678-901		1.20
Germany - Airport Security Tax		18.38
Germany - Airport Service Fees		37.76
Fuel Surcharge		161.00
Total Base Fare (per passenger)		809.39
Number of Passengers		1
TOTAL FARE ⑭	CAD	809.39

Ticket is non-endorsable, non-refundable
Changes allowed, subject to availability,
no later than 2 hours before departure.
Please read carefully all fare restrictions.

Have a pleasant flight!

⑮ Paid by Credit Card XXXX-XXXX-XXXX-1234

(cc by Airodyssey)

① **Booking Number** 預訂代碼
② **Flight Number** 航班號碼
③ **From . . . To . . .** 出發地與目的地
④ **Aircraft Type** 班機型號
⑤ **Airline Class** 航班艙等
⑥ **Seat Status** 座位狀態
⑦ **Time** 出發時間
⑧ **Passenger Name** 旅客姓名
⑨ **Ticket Number** 機票號碼
⑩ **Frequent Flyer Number** 飛行常客號碼
⑪ **Special Needs** 特殊需求
⑫ **Purchase Description** 購買細節
⑬ **Price** 價格
⑭ **Total Fare** 總額
⑮ **Forms of Payment** 付款方式

ELECTRONIC TICKET
PASSENGER ITINERARY/RECEIPT
CUSTOMER COPY

1 Passenger: LI, MEI-HUEI **4** Ticket No: 0015704034215
2 Booking Ref: MFEGXF **5** Issuing Airline: AMERICAN AIRLINES, INC.
3 Frequent Flyer No: **6** Tour Code: AATWAO

7 DATE		**8** CITY/STOPOVER	**9** TIME	**10** FLY/CLS/ST	**11** EQP/FLY TIME	**12** FARE BASIS
15AUG	DEP	TAIPEI TAOYUAN, TPE TERMINAL 2	1000	JL802 ECONOMY (Y)	NON-STOP 788	YNE08YN0/ TW02
15AUG	ARR	TOKYO NARITA TERMINAL 2	1420	OK	03HR20MIN	

13 OPERATED BY JAPAN AIRLINES/JAPAN AIRLINES INTERNATIONAL COMPANY LTD

JAPAN AIRLINES REF:6FBQXK			SEAT:		NVA:15AUG17	BAG:2PC
15AUG	DEP	TOKYO NARITA TERMINAL 2	1830	AA60 ECONOMY (Y)	NON-STOP BOEING 777-200	YNE08YN0/ TW02
15AUG	ARR	DALLAS INTL TERMINAL D	1630	OK	12HR00MIN	

14 OPERATED BY AMERICAN AIRLINES/AMERICAN AIRLINES, INC.

❶ Passenger Name 旅客姓名：
拼法必須與護照姓名相同，否則無法登機，因此機票不可轉讓。

❷ Booking Reference Number 預訂代碼

❸ Frequent Flyer Number 飛行常客號碼

❹ E-Ticket Number 電子機票號碼

❺ Issuing Airline 核發航空

❻ Tour Code 團體代號：用於團體機票

❼ Date 出發日期

❽ City/Stopover 出發與目的城市／中途停留

❾ Time 出發時間

❿ FLY (flight number) / CLS (class) / ST (status)
航班號碼／艙等／狀態

⓫ EQP (equipment) / FLY Time (flying time) 班機型號／飛行時間

⓬ Fare Basis Code 票種代碼

⓭ The airline that takes passengers to the stopover
載旅客前往中途停留點的航空公司

⓮ The airline that takes passengers to the destination
載旅客前往目的地的航空公司

登機證
Boarding Pass

1 **Name of Passenger** 旅客姓名
2 **From . . . to . . .** 出發地與目的地
3 **Flight Number** 班機號碼
4 **Class** 座艙等級
5 **Gate Number** 登機門號碼
6 **Boarding Time** 登機時間
7 **Seat Number** 座位號碼

班機出發時間表
Departure Board

1 **Departure Board**
 班機起飛時間表
2 **Take-Off Time** 起飛時間
3 **Destination** 目的地
4 **Airline Code** 航空代碼
5 **Flight Number** 班機號碼
6 **Boarding Gate** 登機門
7 **Remarks** 備註
8 **Departed** 已起飛
9 **Boarding** 登機中
10 **On Time** 準時
11 **Delayed** 誤點
12 **Cancelled** 取消
13 **New Departure Time**
 已更改時間

有些機場的 departure board 會標示
SCHED-TIME（scheduled-time 預訂起飛時間）
和 EST-TIME（established-time 實際起飛時間）。
備註欄的班機狀態還有可能出現下列訊息：

★ FINAL CALL 最後登機廣播

★ CHECK-IN NOW 辦理登機手續中

★ TIME CHANGE 時間更改

美國簽證
American VISA

① **Issuing Post Name**
   簽證核發地

② **Control Number** 簽證號碼

③ **Surname** 姓

④ **Given Name** 名

⑤ **Visa Type** 簽證種類

   Regular 一般

   Official 公務

   Diplomatic 外交

   Other 其他

⑥ **Class** 艙等

⑦ **Passport Number** 護照號碼

⑧ **Sex** 性別

   M (male) 男 / **F (female)** 女

⑨ **Birth Date** 生日

⑩ **Nationality** 國籍

⑪ **Entries** 入境次數

   M (multiple) 多次入境

   S (single) 單次入境

⑫ **Issue Date** 簽證核發日

⑬ **Expiration Date** 簽證到期日

⑭ **Annotation** 註解

申根簽證
Schengen VISA

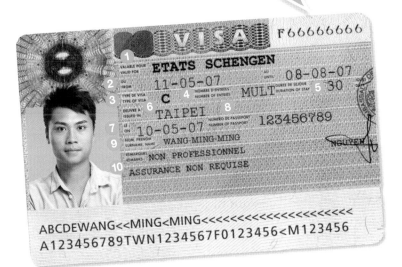

❶ **Valid For** 此證件適用於（申根國家）

❷ **From . . . Until . . .** 簽證有效期限

❸ **Type of Visa** 簽證種類

　C (short term) 短期簽證

　D (long term) 長期簽證

❹ **Number of Entries** 入境次數

　mult 多次入境 / **single** 單次入境

❺ **Duration of Stay** 可停留時間

❻ **Issued In** 簽證辦理處

❼ **On (Date)** 簽證辦理時間

❽ **Number of Passport** 護照號碼

❾ **Surname, Name** 申辦人姓名

❿ **Remarks** 備註

On an Airplane

Chapter

···

2

在飛機上

① **overhead compartment** 頭頂置物艙

④ **aisle** 走道

⑤ **middle seat** 中間的座位

② **window seat** 靠窗座位

③ **aisle seat** 靠走道的座位

⑥ **flight attendant** 空服員

⑦ **crew** 機組人員

⑪ **buckle** 扣帶

⑧ **captain** 機長

⑨ **airsickness bag** 嘔吐袋

⑩ **seat belt** 安全帶

⑫ **blind** 窗戶遮陽板

⑬ **tray** 摺疊餐桌

⑭ **seat pocket** 椅背置物袋

⑮ **headphones/headset** 耳機

⑯ **pillow** 枕頭

⑰ **blanket** 毛毯

⑱ **console**
（電子設備或機器的）
操控臺

⑲ **touch screen** 觸控螢幕；
in-flight entertainment
機上娛樂

20 electronic device
電子產品

21 in-flight meal
機上餐點

22 duty-free items
免稅商品

23 life jacket 救生衣

24 oxygen mask 氧氣罩

25 emergency exit 逃生出口

26 time difference 時差

㉗ **plane cockpit** 飛機駕駛艙

㉘ **economy class** 經濟艙

㉙ **business class** 商務艙

㉚ **first class** 頭等艙

㉛ **in-flight movie** 機上電影

㉜ **lavatory** 洗手間

㉝ **occupied**（洗手間）有人使用

㉞ **vacant**（洗手間）沒人使用

㉟ **turbulence** 亂流

㊱ **vomit / throw up** 嘔吐

㊲ **airsickness** 暈機

㊳ **ringing in the ears** 耳鳴

㊴ **jet lag** 時差反應

㊵ **vegetarian food** 素食

㊶ **beef** 牛肉

㊷ **pork** 豬肉

㊸ **fish** 魚肉

㊹ **bread; roll** 麵包

㊺ **the international date line**
國際換日線

㊻ **altitude** 高度

㊼ **ground temperature** 地面溫度

㊽ **Centigrade** 攝氏溫度（或用 Celsius）

㊾ **Fahrenheit** 華氏溫度

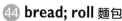

33

❶ Having Lunch on the Plane 在飛機上用餐 (013)

David	What are my choices for lunch?
Flight attendant	We have beef with rice and fish with noodles. Which would you like?
David	Fish with noodles, please.
Flight attendant	Would you care for coffee or tea?
David	Coffee, please.

大衛	午餐有什麼可以選？
空服員	有牛肉飯和鮮魚麵，您要哪一種？
大衛	我要鮮魚麵。
空服員	要不要喝點咖啡或茶呢？
大衛	請給我咖啡。

airsick 暈機

airsickness bag 嘔吐袋

❷ Airsickness 暈機 ⟨014⟩

Flight attendant	May I help you?
Monica	I don't feel well. I need an airsickness bag.
Flight attendant	Yes, madam. There's one in the seat pocket. Here you are.
Monica	Thank you.
Flight attendant	Should I bring you some water?
Monica	Yes, please.

空服員	請問需要什麼嗎？
莫妮卡	我覺得不太舒服，麻煩給我一個嘔吐袋。
空服員	好的，嘔吐袋就在椅背裡，來。
莫妮卡	謝謝！
空服員	需要喝一點水嗎？
莫妮卡	好。

•Pattern Drills

❶ Having Lunch on the Plane 在飛機上用餐 ⟨015⟩

David	What are my choices for lunch?
Flight attendant	We have <u>beef with rice</u> and <u>fish with noodles</u>. Which would you like?
David	<u>Fish with noodles</u>, please.
Flight attendant	<u>Would you care for coffee or tea?</u>
David	<u>Coffee</u>, please.

airline dishes 機上餐

一般長程班機多半會印製菜單,放在座椅口袋內,或在飛機起飛後發
給旅客,供旅客事先考慮想吃哪一種餐點。有些航空公司則是會在訂
購機票時,詢問旅客是否要機上餐,到了機上便不再詢問乘客,而是
直接依登記名冊發送餐點。

吃素的旅客,別忘了在訂機票或辦理登記時告訴航空公司人員,
以便航空人員預先準備你的餐點。

1

pork with rice
chicken with pasta
pork with rice / chicken with pasta
Would you like some coffee or tea?
Orange juice

2

fried rice
fried noodles
fried rice/noodles
What would you like to drink?
Sprite

3

lamb
chicken
lamb/chicken
Would you care for something to drink?
Red wine

4

Make up your own conversation.

② Airsickness 暈機 (016)

Flight attendant	May I help you?
Monica	I don't feel well. I need an airsickness bag.
Flight attendant	Yes, madam. There's one in the seat pocket. Here you are.
Monica	Thank you.
Flight attendant	Should I bring you some water?
Monica	Yes, please.

And in the event of a sudden drop in the market, oxygen masks will drop from above your seats.

1

Do you need any help?

I feel like vomiting.

a barf bag

Do you need any assistance to the lavatory?

2

What can I do for you?

I feel like throwing up.

a sickness bag

Would you like to change your seat over the wings?

3

Is there anything I can do for you?

I feel dizzy and airsick.

a vomit bag

Do you need any special medical attention?

4

Make up your own conversation.

I-94 表格
I-94 Form

I-94 表格為出入美國時所需填寫的入境表格，現已數位化。旅客在入境美國時，只需注意更新自己的 EVUS（Electronic Visa Update System 簽證更新電子系統），並在機上填寫右頁的海關申報表即可。

DEPARTMENT OF HOMELAND SECURITY
U.S. Customs and Border Protection
OMB No. 1651-0111

Admission Number
Welcome to the United States

392923282 18

I-94 Arrival/Departure Record - Instructions

1. This form must be completed by all persons except U.S. Citizens, returning resident aliens, aliens with immigrant visas, and Canadian Citizens visiting or in transit.
2. Type or print legibly with pen in ALL CAPITAL LETTERS. Use English. Do not write on the back of this form.
3. This form is in two parts. Please complete both the Arrival Record (Items 1 through 13) and the Departure Record (Items 14 through 17).
4. When all items are completed, present this form to the CBP Officer.
5. Item 7 - If you are entering the United States by land, enter **LAND** in this space. If you are entering the United States by ship, enter **SEA** in this space.

CBP Form I-94 (10/04)

Admission Number
OMB No. 1651-0111

392923282 18

Arrival Record

6. Family Name
7. First (Given) Name
8. Birth Date (Day/Mo/Yr)
9. Day (D) 10. Mo (M) 11. Yr (Y)
12. Country of Citizenship
13. Sex (Male or Female) 14.
15. Passport Number
16. Airline and Flight Number
17. Country Where You Live
18. City Where You Boarded
19. 0. City Where Visa was Issued
20. Date Issued (Day/Mo/Yr)
21. 2. Address While in the United States (Number and Street)
22. 3. City and State

CBP Form I-94 (10/04)

Departure Number
OMB No. 1651-0111

392923282 18

**I-94
Departure Record**

14. Family Name
15. First (Given) Name
16. Birth Date (Day/Mo/Yr)
17. Country of Citizenship

CBP Form I-94 (10/04)

See Other Side
STAPLE HERE

---

1. This form must be completed by all persons except U.S. citizens, returning resident aliens, aliens with immigrant visas, and Canadian Citizens visiting or in transit. 所有人都必須填寫此表格，除了美國公民、返回美國的永久居民外籍人士、持移民簽證首次入境的新移民外籍人士、入境美國的加拿大公民或是過境的外籍旅客。

2. Type or print legibly with pen in ALL CAPITAL LETTERS. Use English. Do not write on the back of this form. 請用大寫字母打字或用筆填寫清楚，使用英文填寫，不要在此表背面寫任何字。

3. This form is in two parts. Please complete both the Arrival Record (Item 1 through 13) and the Departure Record (Item 14 through 17). 此表包括兩部分，請填寫入境記錄（第 1 項至第 13 項）和離境記錄（第 14 項至第 17 項）兩部分。

4. When all items are completed, present this form to the U.S. Immigration and Naturalization Service Inspector. 填寫完畢後，請將此表交給美國移民局官員。

5. Item 7—If you are entering the United States by land, enter LAND in this space. If you are entering the United States by ship, enter SEA in this space. 第 7 項內容說明——如果您是從陸路進入美國，請在空格內填寫 LAND。如果您是搭乘船隻進入美國，請在空格內填寫 SEA。

6. Family Name 姓氏
7. First (Given) Name 名字
8. Birth Date 生日
9. Day (D) 日
10. Mo (M) 月
11. Yr (Y) 年
12. Country of Citizenship 國籍
13. Sex 性別
14. Male (M) / Female (F) 男性／女性
15. Passport Number 護照號碼
16. Airline and Flight Number 航空公司與航班號碼
17. Country Where You Live 居住國家
18. City Where You Boarded 登機／登船城市
19. City Where Visa Was Issued 簽證核發城市
20. Date Issued 簽證核發時間
21. Address While in the United States (Number and Street) 在美國期間的居住地點（街道與號碼）
22. City and State 城市與州名

海關申報表
Customs Declaration Form

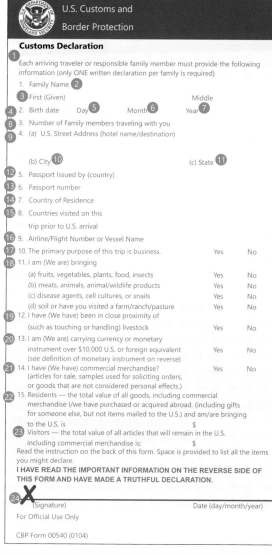

U.S. Customs and Border Protection

Customs Declaration

① Each arriving traveler or responsible family member must provide the following information (only ONE written declaration per family is required)

1. Family Name ②
③ First (Given)   Middle
④ 2. Birth date   Day ⑤   Month ⑥   Year ⑦
⑧ 3. Number of Family members traveling with you
⑨ 4. (a) U.S. Street Address (hotel name/destination)

   (b) City ⑩   (c) State ⑪
⑫ 5. Passport Issued by (country)
⑬ 6. Passport number
⑭ 7. Country of Residence
⑮ 8. Countries visited on this
   trip prior to U.S. arrival
⑯ 9. Airline/Flight Number or Vessel Name
⑰ 10. The primary purpose of this trip is business.   Yes   No
⑱ 11. I am (We are) bringing

   (a) fruits, vegetables, plants, food, insects   Yes   No
   (b) meats, animals, animal/wildlife products   Yes   No
   (c) disease agents, cell cultures, or snails   Yes   No
   (d) soil or have you visited a farm/ranch/pasture   Yes   No
⑲ 12. I have (We have) been in close proximity of
   (such as touching or handling) livestock   Yes   No
⑳ 13. I am (We are) carrying currency or monetary
   instrument over $10,000 U.S. or foreign equivalent
   (see definition of monetary instrument on reverse)   Yes   No
㉑ 14. I have (We have) commercial merchandise?   Yes   No
   (articles for sale, samples used for soliciting orders,
   or goods that are not considered personal effects.)
㉒ 15. Residents — the total value of all goods, including commercial
   merchandise I/we have purchased or acquired abroad. (including gifts
   for someone else, but not items mailed to the U.S.) and am/are bringing
   to the U.S. is $
㉓ Visitors — the total value of all articles that will remain in the U.S.
   including commercial merchandise is: $
Read the instruction on the back of this form. Space is provided to list all the items you might declare.
I HAVE READ THE IMPORTANT INFORMATION ON THE REVERSE SIDE OF THIS FORM AND HAVE MADE A TRUTHFUL DECLARATION.

㉔ **X**
(Signature)   Date (day/month/year)
For Official Use Only

CBP Form 00540 (0104)

① Each arriving traveler or responsible family member must provide the following information (only ONE written declaration per family is required) 每位入境旅客或家庭代表均須填妥下列資料（每個家庭只需填寫一張）

② Family Name 姓

③ First (Given) Name 名

④ Birth Date 生日

⑤ Day 日

⑥ Month 月

⑦ Year 年

⑧ Number of Family members traveling with you 同行家屬人數（不包含自己）

⑨ U.S. Street Address (hotel name/destination) 美國居住地址（飯店／目的地名稱）

⑩ City 城市名

⑪ State 州名

⑫ Passport Issued by (country) 護照發照國家

⑬ Passport number 護照號碼

⑭ Country of Residence 居住國家

⑮ Countries visited on this trip prior to U.S. arrival 此趟行程抵美前，還去過哪些國家

⑯ Airline/Flight Number or Vessel Name 航空公司／班機號碼或船艦名稱

⑰ The primary purpose of this trip is business. 此行主要目的為洽公

⑱ I am (We are) bringing 我攜帶了
(a) fruits, vegetables, plants, food, insects
蔬果、植物、食物、昆蟲
(b) meats, animals, animal/wildlife products 肉品、動物、動物製品
(c) disease agents, cell cultures, or snails
病原體、細胞培養、蝸牛
(d) soil or have you visited a farm/ranch/pasture 土壤，或您曾造訪農場

⑲ I have (We have) been in close proximity of (such as touching or handling) livestock 我（我們）曾經近距離接觸家畜

⑳ I am (We are) carrying currency or monetary instrument over $10,000 U.S. or foreign equivalent 我（我們）攜帶了超過一萬美元或等值貨幣

㉑ I have (We have) commercial merchandise? (articles for sale, samples used for soliciting orders, or goods that are not considered personal effects.) 我（我們）有攜帶商品？（販賣之商品、訂購之樣本等任何非屬私人之物品）

㉒ Residents（美國居民才須填寫）

㉓ Visitors — the total value of all articles that will remain in the U.S. including commercial merchandise（遊客填寫）攜帶商品總值

㉔ 填妥表格後，在此處簽名

Chapter

3

入境／轉機

② **transit lounge** 轉機候機室

① **transit / transfer / change planes**
轉機

③ **transit passenger** 過境旅客

④ **transfer desk / transit counter**
轉機櫃檯

⑤ **immigration control/counter**
入境櫃檯

⑥ **customs declaration form**
關稅申報表

⑦ **arrival lobby** 入境大廳

⑧ **baggage claim tag**
行李提領證

⑨ **liquor** 酒　　⑩ **cigarette** 香菸　　⑪ **airport terminal** 航站大廈

⑫ **baggage claim/carousel** 行李提領處　　⑬ **sightseeing** 觀光

⑭ **on business / on a business trip**
洽公／商務旅行

⑮ **prohibited items** 違禁品

⑯ **stopover/layover** 中途過境停留

⑰ **disembarkation card** 入境卡

⑱ **customs** 海關（要用複數型）

⑲ **get through customs** 通關

⑳ **resident** 居民

㉑ **non-resident** 非居民

㉒ **foreigner** 外國人

㉓ **baggage inspection** 行李查驗

㉔ **Lost and Found Office** 行李遺失招領處

㉕ **declare** 申報（納稅品等）

㉖ **customs inspection** 海關檢查

㉗ **(customs) duty** 關稅

㉘ **duty-free** 免稅的

㉙ **duty-free allowance** 免稅額

㉚ **pay the duty for something** 付……的稅

㉛ **personal effects** 私人物品

㉜ **personal belongings** 私人物品

㉝ **for my own use** 自己要用的

常見的機場標誌
Common Airport Signs

Information ?!

Information Counter 服務台

 Departure

Departure Hall 出境大廳

 Arrival

 ← Gate 20 | Gate 21 →

 Terminal

 **Transfer** →

↑ 🧳 **Bag claim**
🧳 **Baggage hall**

→ **Lift**

← **Check-in**

Customs Control ↗

Customs Inspection 海關查驗處

 Passport Control ↗

Passport Inspection 護照查驗處

DUTY FREE 🎁 →　duty-free shop 免稅商店

baggage inspection 行李查驗

Renting a Wi-Fi Router 租借 Wi-Fi 分享器

USB cable USB 線

Wi-Fi router Wi-Fi分享器

AC adaptor 電源轉接器

SIM card
(subscriber identification card) SIM卡

1 At the Immigration Counter 入境櫃檯 019

Immigration Officer	Passport and disembarkation card, please.
David	Here you are.
Immigration Officer	What is your purpose of visiting?
David	Sightseeing.
Immigration Officer	How long are you staying here?
David	Nine days.
Immigration Officer	All right. Thank you.

入境櫃檯人員	請出示您的護照和入境登記表。
大衛	在這裡。
入境櫃檯人員	你來的目的是什麼？
大衛	我是來觀光的。
入境櫃檯人員	你打算在這裡待幾天？
大衛	九天。
入境櫃檯人員	好的，謝謝！

入境櫃檯通常分為好幾種，外籍旅客必須選擇 Foreigner（外國人）、Non-Citizen（非公民）和 Non-Resident（非居民）這三種窗口，並出示 passport（護照）、ticket（機票）和 disembarkation card（入境卡）。

查驗人員通常會詢問一些旅行目的、停留時間、住宿地點等問題，一一回答後便可通過。

❷ Baggage Inspection 行李檢查 🎧020

Customs Officer	Please bring your baggage here for inspection.
Amy	Here you are, officer.
Customs Officer	Is all your baggage here?
Amy	Yes, a camera bag, a travel bag, and a suitcase.
Customs Officer	Have you got anything to declare?
Amy	No. I have only personal effects.

海關人員	請把你的行李拿過來檢查。
艾美	好的，先生。
海關人員	你所有的行李都在這裡了嗎？
艾美	是的，一個相機包、一個旅行袋和一個行李箱。
海關人員	有什麼要申報的嗎？
艾美	沒有，我只有一些私人用品。

❶ At the Immigration Counter 入境櫃檯

Immigration Officer	Passport and disembarkation card, please.
David	Here you are.
Immigration Officer	What is your purpose of visiting?
David	Sightseeing.
Immigration Officer	How long are you staying here?
David	Nine days.
Immigration Officer	All right. Thank you.

1

Passport, please.

I'm here on business.

How many days are you staying here?

One week.

2

Please give me your passport.

I'm here for study.

How long will you be here?

Three months.

3

Please give me your disembarkation card, and let me see your passport.

I'm here on vacation.

What is the duration of your vacation?

Two weeks.

4

Make up your own conversation.

❷ Baggage Inspection 行李檢查 ⟨022⟩

Customs Officer　Please bring your baggage here for inspection.

Amy　Here you are, officer.

Customs Officer　Is all your baggage here?

Amy　Yes, a camera bag, a travel bag, and a suitcase.

Customs Officer　Have you got anything to declare?

Amy　No. I have only personal effects.

有些機場的行李推車（baggage trolley）需要付費才能使用

1
bring your luggage here
a small backpack and a suitcase
Do you have anything to declare?
No. I have only personal belongings.

2
show your baggage
a laptop bag and a four-wheel suitcase
Got any tobacco?
I have a carton of cigarettes, just for my own use.

3
place your baggage here
a carry-on bag and a suitcase with wheels
Anything to declare?
Yes. This watch is a gift for a friend.

4

Make up your own conversation.

Money Exchange

Chapter

4

兑换外幣

1 currency/money exchange 外幣兌換

2 dollar ($) 美金

3 I dollar 美金一元

4 half dollar = 50 cents
美金五十分

5 quarter = 25 cents
美金二十五分

6 dime = 10 cents
美金十分

(024)

7 nickel = 5 cents 美金五分

8 penny = 1 cent 美金一分

9 euro (€) 歐元

10 euro cent 歐分

11 exchange rate 匯率

12 small change 小面額硬幣；零錢

13 sign (v.) 簽名

14 traveler's check 旅行支票

15 bank 銀行

16 ATM
= Automatic Teller Machine
自動提款機

17 window 辦理窗口

⑱ **withdraw** 提款

⑲ **receipt** 收據

 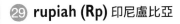 ㉙ **rupiah (Rp)** 印尼盧比亞

⑳ **bill** 紙鈔

㉑ **coin** 硬幣

 ㉚ **rupee (Rs)** 印度盧比

㉒ **banking hours** 營業時間

㉓ **commission /
service charge** 手續費

 ㉛ **baht (B)** 泰銖

㉔ **application form** 申請單

㉕ **New Taiwan dollar
(NT$)** 新台幣

 ㉜ **won (₩)** 韓元

㉖ **pound (£)** 英鎊

㉗ **yen (¥)** 日圓

 ㉝ **ruble (RUB)** 俄羅斯盧布

㉘ **Australian dollar ($)** 澳幣

 ㉞ **rand (R)** 南非蘭特

❶ Where can I change some money?
在哪裡可以換錢？

Timmy	Could you please tell me where I can change some money?
Ann	Over there at the bank.
Timmy	Thanks.

[At the bank]

Timmy	Excuse me, which window is the foreign exchange section?
Service	Please go to window 8.
Timmy	Thank you.

提米	請問我可以到哪裡換錢？
安	到那邊的銀行。
提米	謝謝。

〔走進銀行〕

提米	請問哪一個窗口可以兌換外幣？
服務人員	請到 8 號窗口辦理。
提米	謝謝！

currency exchange counter
外匯兌換櫃檯

❷ I'd like to change US dollars into euros.
我想把美金換成歐元。 028

Timmy	I'd like to change some US dollars into euros and I'd like to know today's exchange rate.
Service	According to today's exchange rate, one US dollar is equivalent to 0.75 euros in cash.
Timmy	Is there any service charge?
Service	We charge a €1 commission on each transaction. How much would you like to change?
Timmy	400 US dollars. Here it is. Would you please give me small bills?
Service	No problem.

提米	我想把這些美金換成歐元,請問今天的匯率是多少?
櫃員	根據外匯牌價,今天是一美元兌換 0.75 歐元。
提米	要付手續費嗎?
櫃員	每筆交易的手續費是一歐元。您想換多少?
提米	四百美元,給你。麻煩換小鈔給我好嗎?
櫃員	好的。

❶ Where can I change some money?

在哪裡可以換錢？ 🎧029

Timmy	Could you please tell me where I can change some money?
Ann	Over there at the bank.
Timmy	Thanks.

[At the bank]

Timmy	Excuse me, which window is the foreign exchange section?
Service	Please go to window 8.
Timmy	Thank you.

to withdraw money 領錢

small euro change 小額歐元零錢

1

Where is the Currency Exchange?
Next to the Tourist Information Center.
can I change some money here?
Sure.

2

Where is the nearest bank?
Right at the corner of this street.
where can I change money?
Please go to money exchange counter.

3

Where can I change some money?
You can change at the hotel front desk.
I want to change some money.
Please change with our cashier.

4

Make up your own conversation.

❷ I'd like to change US dollars into euros.

我想把美金換成歐元。 030

Timmy	I'd like to change some US dollars into euros, and I'd like to know today's exchange rate.
Service	According to today's exchange rate, one US dollar is equivalent to 0.75 euros in cash.
Timmy	Is there any service charge?
Service	We charge a €1 commission on each transaction. How much would you like to change?
Timmy	400 US dollars. Here it is. Would you please give me small bills?
Service	No problem.

旅行支票是一種預先印刷的、具固定金額的支票，持有人需預先支付給發出者（通常是銀行）相對應的金額。旅行支票如果遺失或被盜，可以補發，旅行者能夠在旅行時換取當地貨幣。

旅行者在購買旅行支票後，得先在支票上方欄位預先簽名，之後於購物或是兌換實體貨幣時，再於下方欄簽上自己的名字，收取支票者就會核對上下欄的名字是否相同，以防他人盜用。

現在，因為信用卡、ATM 已經廣泛使用，所以旅行支票的重要地位已經不如從前，接受旅行支票的店家的數量逐年遞減，支票持有者僅能到銀行兌換為當地貨幣使用。甚者，旅行支票最大的發行銀行美國運通（American Express），已經於 2007 年終止旅行支票卡的業務。

1

I want to change some US dollars into euros.
I want to know today's exchange rate.
What is the service charge?
I'll change 100 US dollars.

2

I would like to exchange my US dollars for euros.
What's the exchange rate for euros?
What commission do you charge?
300 US dollars.

3

I'd like to change US dollars into euros.
What is the exchange rate between the US dollar and the euro today?
How much is the commission?
500 US dollars.

4

Make up your own conversation.

Taking a Taxi

Chapter

5

搭計程車

① **call a taxi** 打電話叫車

② **catch a taxi** 攔計程車

③ **taxi stand** 計程車招呼站

④ **meter** 計費表

⑤ **safety belt** 安全帶

⑥ **vacant** 空車

⑦ **trunk** 後行李廂

⑧ **fare** 車資
(basic fare 基本費)

⑨ **keep the change**
不用找錢

⑩ **traffic lights** 紅綠燈　　⑪ **intersection** 十字路口　　⑫ **sidewalk** 人行道

⑬ **crosswalk** 斑馬線　　⑭ **taxi driver** 計程車司機　　⑮ **taxi app** 叫車應用程式

⑯ **front seat** 前座　　⑰ **back seat** 後座　　⑱ **traffic jam** 塞車

⑲ **cab/taxi** 計程車　　　　　　　　㉕ **address** 地址

⑳ **pick up** 接 (乘客) 上車　　　　㉖ **slow down** 放慢速度

㉑ **drop** 放 (乘客) 下車　　　　　㉗ **speed up** 加快速度

㉒ **step in / get in** 上車　　　　　㉘ **take a short cut** 抄捷徑

㉓ **get out of / get off** 下車　　　㉙ **ride** 車程

㉔ **destination** 目的地　　　　　　㉚ **surcharge** 加收費用

❶ Where to, madam? 小姐，要去哪裡？ (033)

Driver	Where to, madam?
Peggy	Grand Central Station, please. I want to catch a 6 p.m. train.
Driver	I think you'll make it if we don't get stuck in a traffic jam.

[After a while]

Driver	Here is Grand Central Station.
Peggy	Thank you. How much is the fare?
Driver	The meter reads $9.15.
Peggy	Here you are. Keep the change.
Driver	Thank you.

司機	小姐，要去哪裡？
珮琪	請到中央車站，我要趕晚上6點的火車。
司機	如果不塞車的話，應該趕得上。

〔過了一會兒〕

司機	中央車站到了。
珮琪	謝謝，多少錢？
司機	9.15 元
珮琪	這是車資，不用找了。
司機	謝謝。

❷ **To this place, please.** 到這裡。（指著地址說）

Driver	Where to, sir?
Peter	To this place, please.
Driver	Star Hotel. OK.
Peter	How long does it take to get to the hotel?
Driver	About 20 minutes.

[After a while]

Driver	Here's the hotel.
Peter	How much is the fare?
Driver	That's $10.

司機	請問要到哪裡？
彼得	到這個地方。〔拿飯店名稱和地址給司機看〕
司機	晨星飯店呀，沒問題。
彼得	車程大概多久？
司機	大概 20 分鐘。

〔過了一會兒〕

司機	飯店到了。
彼得	多少錢？
司機	10 元。

taxi sign 計程車出租燈

•Pattern Drills

1 **Where to, madam?** 小姐，要去哪裡？

Driver	Where to, madam?
Peggy	Grand Central Station, please. I want to catch a 6 p.m. train.
Driver	I think you'll make it if we don't get stuck in a traffic jam.
	[After a while]
Driver	Here is Grand Central Station.
Peggy	Thank you. How much is the fare?
Driver	The meter reads $9.15.
Peggy	Here you are. Keep the change.
Driver	Thank you.

taxi meter 計程車計費表／跳表機

1

| Where do you want to go? |
| Take me to Central Park, please. I'm in a hurry. |
| Here's Central Park. |
| How much do I owe you? |
| $7.80. |

2

| Where are you going? |
| Take me to this place, please. |
| Here you are. |
| How much is it? |
| $12.50. |

3

| Where would you like to go? |
| To this address, please. |
| We are there. |
| What is the charge? |
| $4.50. |

4

Make up your own conversation.

❷ To this place, please. 到這裡。(指著地址說) 036

Driver — Where to, sir?

Peter — To this place, please.

Driver — Star Hotel. OK.

Peter — How long does it take to get to the hotel?

Driver — About 20 minutes.

[After a while]

Driver — Here's the hotel.

Peter — How much is the fare?

Driver — That's $10.

1

| Grand Hyatt Hotel |
| How long is the ride from here? |
| an hour |
| $25 |

2

| Plaza Hotel |
| How long will it take? |
| 15 minutes |
| $12 |

3

| the Wardolf Astoria Hotel |
| Will it take long to get there? |
| 5 minutes |
| $12.50 |

4

Make up your own conversation.

Calling a Taxi With a Smartphone App
用手機叫計程車 🎧037

G *Guest* 乘客　　R *Receptionist* 總機

G　Could you call me a taxi?

R　Do you know about our city's taxi app?

G　No, I don't. Could you tell me about it?

R　It's a free app that allows you to call a taxi from anywhere in the city.

G　How do I use it?

R　It's very simple. Just download the app on your smartphone.

G　OK. Done.

R　Now you need to enter your credit card details and destination.

G　And after that?

R　Just tap on "Call a Taxi" and a nearby taxi will come to pick you up.

G　妳可以幫我叫一台計程車嗎？

R　您知道我們市內的計程車叫車程式嗎？

G　不，我不知道。可以跟我說更詳細嗎？

R　這是一款免費的應用程式，可以讓您在本市內任何地方叫車。

G　要怎麼使用呢？

R　非常簡單。只要在您的智慧型手機上下載程式。

G　好，下好了。

R　接著您需要輸入信用卡資訊，與您的目的地。

G　然後呢？

R　只要按下「立即叫車」的按鈕，位於附近的計程車就會前來接您。

如何使用叫車應用程式
How to Use a Taxi App

1 open your taxi app
打開叫車應用程式

2 enter username and password
輸入帳號和密碼

3 type in address of destination
輸入目的地地址

4 select a vehicle option
選擇車種

5 tap "call" to schedule a ride
按下「叫車」預訂行程

6 done 叫車完成

Traveling by Train

Chapter

....

6

搭乘火車或地鐵

① **railroad station** 火車站　② **platform** 月台　③ **track** 鐵軌

④ **route map** 路線圖

⑤ **timetable** 火車時刻表

Liverpool - Nottingham - Norwich

Service operated by	CT	CT	CT	CT	CT	CT	CT	CT	CT
	◇	◇	◇	◇	◇	◇	◇	◇	◇
Liverpool Lime Street				12.50	13.52	14.52	15.52	16.52	17.52
Warrington Central				13.16	14.18	15.18	16.18	17.18	18.18
Manchester Piccadilly			12.44	13.43	14.44	15.43	16.43	17.43	18.43
Stockport			12.54	13.54	14.54	15.54	16.55	17.54	18.56
Sheffield		12.52	13.58	14.41	15.39	16.39	17.39	18.40	19.37
Chesterfield		13.06	14.13	14.56	15.54	16.53	17.53	18.54	19.53
Nottingham	12.32	13.44	14.54	15.48	16.40	17.38	18.46	19.34	20.35
Grantham	13.14	14.20		16.24	17.24	18.18	19.22		21.19
Peterborough	13.43	14.56	16.05	17.00	17.53	18.55	19.55		21.55
Ely	14.28	15.38	16.41	17.39	18.35	19.32	20.31		22.31
Thetford	14.49	15.59	17.02	18.00	18.56	19.55	20.52		22.52
Norwich	15.28	16.37	17.35	18.35	19.29	20.28	21.25		23.35

⑥ **ticket window** 售票口　⑦ **ticket** 車票　⑧ **ticket stub** 票根

⑨ **express** 快車

⑩ **ticket machine** 自動售票機

⑪ **gate** 剪票口

⑫ **locker** 寄物櫃

⑬ **train car** 車廂

⑭ **conductor** 列車掌

⑮ **dining car** 餐車

⑯ **first-class** 頭等車廂

⑰ **sleeper** 臥舖車

⑱ **catch the train** 趕火車

⑲ **ticket office** 售票處

⑳ **reserve a seat** 劃位

㉑ **fare** 票價

㉒ **one-way ticket** (US) 單程票（美國）

㉓ **round-trip ticket** (US) 來回票（美國）

㉔ **single ticket** (UK) 單程票（英國）

㉕ **return ticket** (UK) 來回票（英國）

㉖ **refund the ticket** 退票

㉗ **change trains** 換車

㉘ **train type** 車種

㉙ **through/nonstop train** 直達車

㉚ **stopping/local train** 慢車（每站停的車）

㉛ **full** 客滿

㉜ **line** 鐵路線

㉝ **car** (US) / **coach** (UK) 普通車廂（美國／英國）

㉞ **aisle seat** 靠走道的座位

㉟ **window seat** 靠窗的座位

㊱ **excursion** 短程旅行

❶ Traveling by Train in England 在英國搭火車

Peter	Good morning. Could you tell me the departure times of trains to London, please?
Booking clerk	Yes. There are trains departing at 7:59, 9:18, and 10:32.
Peter	What time does the 7:59 train get to London?
Booking clerk	At 9:36.
Peter	What about coming back? I'd like to come back at about 7 p.m.
Booking clerk	There's one at 7:10 p.m., and the next one is at 7:40 p.m.
Peter	OK, how much is a return ticket?
Booking clerk	If you get on before 4 p.m. or after 6 p.m., there is a saver return which is £9. An ordinary return is £16.
Peter	An ordinary return, please.

彼得	早安。請告訴我去倫敦的火車發車時間。
售票員	好的。7 點 59 分、9 點 18 分和 10 點 32 分各有一班。
彼得	7 點 59 分的火車幾點到達倫敦？
售票員	9 點 36 分。
彼得	回程的時間呢？我想在晚上 7 點左右回來。
售票員	晚上 7 點 10 分有一班，再下一班是 7 點 40 分。
彼得	好，來回票多少錢？
售票員	如果您在下午 4 點之前或 6 點之後上車，有優專票價 9 英鎊的當天來回票。普通來回票要 16 英鎊。
彼得	請給我普通來回票。

❷ Traveling by Train in America 在美國搭火車 (041)

Adam	What time does the train for Boston leave?
Booking clerk	9:25 on Platform 12, Track B.
Adam	When does it arrive?
Booking clerk	It should be there at 11:45, but it may be a little late.
Adam	How much is a one-way ticket?
Booking clerk	It's $32.00.

亞當	去波士頓的火車什麼時候開？
售票員	9 點 25 分，在 12 月台，軌道 B。
亞當	什麼時候抵達波士頓？
售票員	應該是 11 點 45 分到，不過有時候會誤點。
亞當	單程車票一張多少錢？
售票員	32 美元。

如果你打算在美國做短途旅行，建議你可以搭乘火車。坐火車可以避免繁瑣的安檢，另一方面空間也比較大，並且可以使用手機和筆記本電腦，有些車廂甚至安裝有電源插頭。而且，坐火車還可能比搭乘飛機便宜而且省時。

Amtrak 是美國國家鐵路客運公司，是十分穩靠的交通工具，提供相當完善的服務。可以在行程前先上 Amtrak 網站（www.amtrak.com）查看時刻表。

Amtrak 美國國鐵

•Pattern Drills

❶ Traveling by Train in England 在英國搭火車

Peter	Good morning. Could you tell me the departure times of trains to London, please?
Booking clerk	Yes. There are trains departing at 7:59, 9:18, and 10:32.
Peter	What time does the 7:59 train get to London?
Booking clerk	At 9:36.
Peter	What about coming back? I'd like to come back at about 7 p.m.
Booking clerk	There's one at 7:10 p.m., and the next one is at 7:40 p.m.
Peter	OK, how much is a return ticket?
Booking clerk	If you get on before 4 p.m. or after 6 p.m., there is a saver return which is £9. An ordinary return is £16.
Peter	An ordinary return, please.

schedule board 時刻表

1

Trains are departing
9:18
It's due in at noon.
A saver return, please.

2

The departure times of trains are
10:32
It's scheduled to arrive at 1:09 p.m.
An ordinary return ticket, please.

3

Trains are scheduled
next
It's scheduled to arrive at 9:36.
A cheaper ticket, please.

4

Make up your own conversation.

❷ Traveling by Train in America 在美國搭火車 ⟨043⟩

Adam	What time does the train for Boston leave?
Booking clerk	9:25 on Platform 12, Track B.
Adam	When does it arrive?
Booking clerk	It should be there at 11:45, but it may be a little late.
Adam	How much is a one-way ticket?
Booking clerk	It's $32.00.

如果你要搭乘地鐵或捷運，所需的會話基本上和火車一樣。❶在美國及澳洲，地鐵稱為 subway（洛杉磯稱 Metro），❷在英國稱為 underground 或 tube，❸在法國稱為 Metro（上車時必須自己拉桿或按鈕才會開門）。

有些地方的地鐵會發行一日票、週票或月票，長時間待在某地的旅客也可以購買這類車票。

歐美許多國家在通過驗票口時，乘客通常只需將票卡插入驗票機，機器會自動驗票。搭乘火車途中，則會有車掌一一驗票，請務必將票根保留。

1

When is the next train to New York?
Platform 1
When does it get there?
round-trip ticket
It will cost you $32.

2

What time does the next train for Los Angeles leave?
the platform at the left
What time does it get there?
single ticket
You need to pay $32.

3

Which train do I take to Miami?
East platform
What time does it arrive there?
return ticket
The ticket price is $32.

4

Make up your own conversation.

Renting a Car

7

租車

1 **rent a car** 租車

2 **international driver's license / international driving permit** 國際駕照

3 **rate** 費用

4 **try (it)** 試車

5 **check in / return** 歸還車子
⟷ **check out** 租走車子

6 **compact** 小型車

7 **SUV = sport utility vehicle** 休旅車

8 **van** 箱型車

9 **speed limit** 速限

10 **police officer** 警察

11 **parking space** 停車位

12 **parking lot** 停車場

⑬ **parking meter** 停車計費表

⑭ **one-way** 單行道的；單向的

⑮ **No U-turn** 禁止迴轉

⑯ **road map** 地圖

⑰ **scrape/scratch** 刮痕

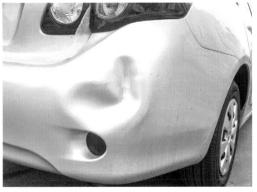

⑱ **dent** 凹痕

(047)

Chap. 7 租車

PART ❶ Key Terms

⑲ **automatic car** 自排車

⑳ **manual car** 手排車

㉑ **start a car** 發動車子

㉒ **mileage** 哩程數

㉓ **under construction** 道路施工

㉔ **be broken down** 拋錨

㉕ **flat tire** 爆胎

㉖ **deposit / security hold** 押金

㉗ **rental agreement** 租車合約

㉘ **insurance** 保險

㉙ **full insurance/coverage** 全險

㉚ **Personal Accident Insurance** (PAI) 個人意外險

㉛ **Personal Effects Protection** (PEP) 攜帶物品險

㉜ **Low Protection** (LP) 強制險

㉝ **Theft Protection** (TP) 竊盜險

㉞ **Loss Damage Waiver** (LDW) = **Collision Damage Waiver** (CDW) 碰撞險（發生車禍導致汽車毀損時，可免除負擔賠償金）

㉟ **walk-through** 檢視車子是否有毀損

㊱ **dead end** 此路不通

93

❶ I'd like to rent a car. 我想租車。 🎧048

Victor	I'd like to rent a car.
Car Rental	May I see your driver's license, please?
Victor	Here is my international driver's license. What kinds of cars do you have?
Car Rental	We have Honda, Citroen, and Toyota. Which make and model do you prefer?
Victor	I'll take the Citroen C2. What is the rate for the car per day?
Car Rental	The price is €60 per day. Do you want insurance?
Victor	Full coverage, please.
Car Rental	That's an extra €10 a day.
Victor	Do I have to fill up the tank when I check in?
Car Rental	Yes.

維多	我想要租車。
租車行	請出示您的駕照好嗎？
維多	這是我的國際駕照。你們有什麼車？
租車行	我們有本田、雪鐵龍和豐田的車，你想要哪一種？
維多	那我要租雪鐵龍的 C2。租金一天多少？
租車行	一天 60 歐元。你要不要保險？
維多	我要加全險。
租車行	那一天要多加 10 歐元。
維多	我還車的時候需要把油加滿嗎？
租車行	要。

❷ The car isn't running smoothly.

車子開起來不太順。 🎧049

Anna	The car isn't running smoothly. I'd like to have a look at it.
Victor	What's the matter with it?
Anna	I'm not sure. It could be the tires. Let's stop here.
Victor	Is there something wrong with the tires?
Anna	It's nothing serious. The right one just needs some air.

安娜	車子開起來不大對勁,我想檢查一下。
維多	出了什麼毛病?
安娜	不清楚。有可能是輪胎出問題,我們先在這裡停一下。
維多	輪胎怎麼樣?
安娜	沒什麼大問題,右邊輪胎需要充氣。

•Pattern Drills

❶ I'd like to rent a car. 我想租車。 🎧050

Victor	I'd like to rent a car.
Car Rental	May I see your driver's license, please?
Victor	Here is my international driver's license. What kinds of cars do you have?
Car Rental	We have Honda, Citroen, and Toyota. Which make and model do you prefer?
Victor	I'll take the Citroen C2. What is the rate for the car per day?
Car Rental	The price is €60 per day. Do you want insurance?
Victor	Full coverage, please.
Car Rental	That's an extra €10 a day.
Victor	Do I have to fill up the tank when I check in?
Car Rental	Yes.

PART

3

Pattern Drills

1

What kind of car would you like?
Honda CIVIC
What is the rate?
€60 per day

2

What type of car would you like?
Toyota Corolla Altis
How much does it cost?
€400 per week

3

What model do you want?
Citroen C4
How much is the daily rental?
€70 per day

4

Make up your own conversation.

❷ The car isn't running smoothly.
車子開起來不太順。 🎧051

Anna The car isn't running smoothly. I'd like to have a look at it.

Victor What's the matter with it?

Anna I'm not sure. It could be the tires. Let's stop here.

Victor Is there something wrong with the tires?

Anna It's nothing serious. The right one just needs some air.

checking the tire pressure
檢查胎壓

pumping air into the tire 打氣

PART

3

Pattern Drills

1

The car makes strange noises.
What's wrong with the car?
It might be the engine.
How is the engine?
The car is hard to start.

2

There is something wrong with the brakes.
What's the matter with it?
The brakes cannot hold well.
How are the brakes?
I called somebody to tow it away.

3

The car has a problem.
What's wrong?
I've got a flat tire.
How are the tires?
The left tire needs to be changed.

4

Make up your own conversation.

汽車構造
Car Parts

windshield 擋風玻璃

side/wing mirror 後照鏡

windshield wiper 雨刷

trunk 後行李箱

hood 車蓋

headlight 車燈

tire 輪胎

signal light 方向燈

license plate 車牌

bumper 保險桿

steering wheel 方向盤

emergency brake 手煞車

gauge 儀表

dashboard 儀錶板

horn 喇叭

gear 排檔桿

driver's seat 駕駛座

passenger seat 副駕駛座

back seat 後座

child safety seat
兒童安全座椅

rear-view mirror 後視鏡

GPS (global positioning system) 導航系統

exhaust pipe 排氣管

engine 引擎

battery 電瓶

jumper cables 救車線

emergency warning triangle 三角警示牌

traffic cone 交通錐

如果要租車，建議在出發前先上網或是打電話訂車，車商就會在約定的時間，將車子送到指定地點或機場。

需特別注意，在英、紐澳等國開車是右座駕駛（right-hand drive），不同於國內的左駕（left-hand drive），開車時要特別小心。租車前建議先試車，並檢查車子本身是否有刮痕或受損，這些都須在事前先跟車行人員說清楚。若真的發生事故，該由哪一方承擔責任，也都必須先當面談清，以免事後衍生更多問題。

出示駕照	**1**	May I see your international driving permit? 請出示您的國際駕照好嗎？
詢問租金	**2**	What is the rate for the car per day? 一天的租金是多少？
	3	How much is the daily rental? 一天的租金是多少？
	4	Could you show me the rate list? 有沒有價目表可以看？
押金	**5** Ⓐ	How much is the deposit? 押金要多少？
	Ⓑ	There is a $500 deposit. 需要 500 美元的押金。
保險費	**6**	Does this include insurance? 這個價錢有含保險費嗎？
全險	**7**	Full coverage, please. 我要保全險。
意外險	**8**	I would like the accident insurance. 我要保意外險。
加滿油	**9**	Do I have to fill up when I check in? 我還車時需要把油加滿嗎？
哩程數限制	**10**	Is the mileage free? 開車哩程數不計費嗎？
	11	Is there any mileage limit? 開車哩程數有限制嗎？
	12	What is the charge per mile? 哩程數怎麼收費？

路標
Road Signs

STOP
停車再開

DO NOT ENTER
禁止進入

YIELD
讓道

DETOUR
繞道

RAILROAD CROSSING
鐵路平交道

DEAD END
此路不通

ONE WAY
單行道

INTERSTATE ROUTE
州際公路

U.S. ROUTE
美國國道

MINIMUM SPEED
最低速限

SPEED LIMIT
最高速限

DO NOT PASS
禁止通行

NO U-TURN
禁止迴轉

NO LEFT TURN
禁止左轉

NO RIGHT TURN
禁止右轉

NO MOTOR VEHICLES
禁止汽機車通行

(cc by Ywang.tw)

國際駕照（International Driving Permit）申辦

若要出國自駕，務必要在出國前先辦好國際駕照，申辦方式如下：

★ 換國際駕照所需證件：
　① 身分證或居留證正本
　　（若為代委託辦理，則請代辦人攜帶雙證件）
　② 原駕照正本
　③ 2 吋半身照片 2 張
　④ 護照影本（用以查核英文姓名及出生地）

★ 申辦費用：250 元

★ 申辦地點：監理站的「駕照綜合窗口」

Finding the Way

Chapter

....

8

問路

1 **landmark** 地標

2 **lose one's way** 迷路

3 **direction** 方向

4 **ask for directions** 問路

5 **city map** 市區地圖

6 **traffic lights** 紅綠燈

7 **block** 街區

8 **at the corner** 在轉角

9 **cross the street** 過馬路

10 **public restroom/toilet** 公共廁所

11 **on your left** 在你的左手邊

13 **on your right** 在你的右手邊

12 **go straight** 直走

14 **navigation app** 導航應用程式

15 **sign** (n.) 標牌；標誌

16 **address** 地址

17 **road** 道路

18 **area** 地區

19 **location** 位置

20 **mark** 標誌

21 **look for** 尋找

22 **miss** 錯過

23 **building** 建築物

24 **across/opposite** 在……對面

25 **head** (v.) 前往

26 **on foot** 步行

❶ Could you tell me the way to . . . ?

請問去……怎麼走？

Vicky	Excuse me. Could you tell me the way to the Star Hotel?
Peter	Yes. Go down the main road. You can't miss it.
Vicky	How long will it take me to get there?
Peter	It's only about a five-minute walk.
Vicky	Thank you very much.
Peter	You're welcome.

薇琪	不好意思，請問晨星飯店怎麼走？
彼得	喔，沿著大路往前走，就可以找到。
薇琪	到那裡大概要多久？
彼得	只要走五分鐘左右。
薇琪	非常感謝。
彼得	不用客氣。

❷ I think I'm lost here. 我想我迷路了。

Vincent	Good morning, madam. I think I'm lost here. The place I want to go to is a hotel called The Hilton.
Annie	Do you know in which area?
Vincent	No, I am sorry I have no idea. I am a stranger here.
Annie	I see. Well, do you know anything near the hotel?
Vincent	Oh, yes. My friend told me the hotel was near the Central Railway Station.
Annie	Then you'll have to take a bus and get off at the Central Railway Station.
Vincent	Can you show me where the Central Railway Station is on this map?
Annie	OK.

文森	小姐早安。我想我迷路了，我要去希爾頓大飯店。
安妮	你知道是在哪一個地區嗎？
文森	對不起，我不知道，我沒有來過這裡。
安妮	這樣啊。那你知道飯店附近有什麼地標嗎？
文森	知道，我朋友說是在中央火車站附近。
安妮	那麼你就坐公車到中央火車站下車。
文森	可不可以請妳指給我看，中央火車站在地圖上的什麼地方呢？
安妮	可以啊。

❶ Could you tell me the way to . . . ?
請問去……怎麼走？

Vicky　Excuse me. Could you tell me the way to the Star Hotel?

Peter　Yes. Go down the main road. You can't miss it.

Vicky　How long will it take me to get there?

Peter　It's only about a five-minute walk.

Vicky　Thank you very much.

Peter　You're welcome.

city map

1

Louvre Museum
It's two blocks straight ahead.
five minutes
Thanks a lot.

2

Central Park
Go straight back down this street.
a three-minute walk
I appreciate your help.

3

the City Zoo
Please go to the end of this road.
a ten-minute walk away
Thank you for your assistance.

4

Make up your own conversation.

❷ I think I'm lost here. 我想我迷路了。 (057)

Vincent Good morning, madam. I think I'm lost here. The place I want to go to is a hotel called The Hilton.

Annie Do you know in which area?

Vincent No, I am sorry I have no idea. I am a stranger here.

Annie I see. Well, do you know anything near the hotel?

Vincent Oh, yes. My friend told me the hotel was near the Central Railway Station.

Annie Then you'll have to take a bus and get off at the Central Railway Station.

Vincent Can you show me where the Central Railway Station is on this map?

Annie OK.

1

| I wonder if you can help me. |
| the Statue of Liberty |
| sculpture |
| New York Harbor |
| **New York Harbor** |

2

| I think I lost my way. |
| the National Concert Hall |
| concert hall |
| Chiang Kai-shek Memorial Hall |
| **Chiang Kai-shek Memorial Hall Station** |

3

| I'm lost. |
| Taipei World Trade Center |
| center |
| Taipei 101 |
| **Taipei 101 Station** |

4

Make up your own conversation.

At the Gas Station

Chapter

9

加油站

058

① gas station (US) **/ petrol station** (UK)
加油站（美／英）

② gas gauge 油錶

③ run out of gas 沒油了

④ regular 普通汽油

⑤ unleaded 無鉛汽油

⑥ premium 高級汽油

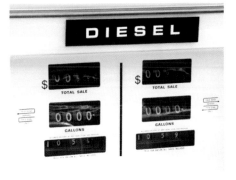

⑦ **diesel** 柴油　　　　　⑧ **insert** 插入

⑨ **gas pump** 加油機　　　　⑩ **gas pump nozzle** 油槍

⑪ **gas/fuel tank** 油箱

⑫ **gas tank door** 油箱門　　　⑬ **gas tank cap** 油箱蓋

⑭ **self-service gas station** 自助式加油站

⑮ **full-service gas station** 有站務員服務的加油站

⑯ **oil** 機油

⑰ **gallon** 加侖（ **liter** 公升）

⑱ **press the button** 按按鈕

061

⑳ **handle** 把手

㉒ **nozzle** 油槍嘴

㉑ **trigger** 加油扳機

⑲ **gas hose** 油槍管

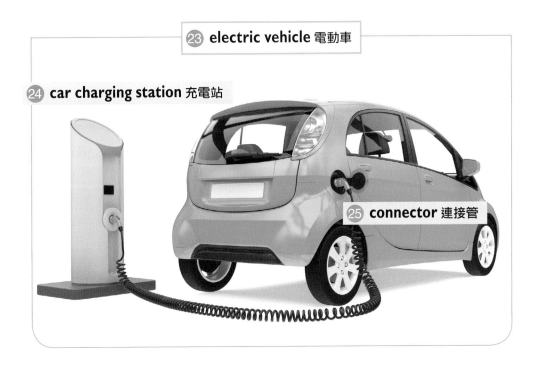

㉓ **electric vehicle** 電動車

㉔ **car charging station** 充電站

㉕ **connector** 連接管

㉖ **fill up something** 將……加滿；填滿

㉗ **select the gas** 選擇汽油

㉘ **release** 釋放

㉙ **nearby** 附近

㉚ **come to
(the total amount of money)**
共……元

❶ At the Full-Service Gas Station 請站務員加油 🎧062

Victor	We're running out of gas. How far is the nearest gas station?
Amy	It's only a few kilometers to the nearest gas station.

[Five minutes later]

Victor	Fill it up, please.
Attendant	What kind of gas would you like?
Victor	Regular, please.
Attendant	OK.
Victor	How much is that?
Attendant	It comes to $50.

維多	我們快沒油了，最近的加油站還有多遠？
艾美	再開幾公里就到了。

gas station attendant 加油站站務員

〔五分鐘後〕

維多	請加滿。
站務員	要加哪一種油？
維多	普通汽油。
站務員	好的。
維多	多少錢？
站務員	總共 50 元。

❷ At the Self-Service Gas Station 在自助加油站

Phoebe	Excuse me. Can you tell me how to fill up the gas tank?
Harry	Of course. First, run the credit card through the machine, and select the gas you'd like.
Phoebe	What should I do after that?
Harry	Insert the nozzle into the tank of your car. Be careful, the gas hose is very heavy. Now press the button on the pump to allow the gas to flow, and pull the trigger on the handle of the gas hose. The gas will be released into the tank of your car. When the tank is full, the fuel will stop pumping.
Phoebe	Sounds easy! Thank you.

菲碧	不好意思，你可不可以教我怎麼加油？
哈利	可以啊。先刷卡並選擇你要哪一種油。
菲碧	然後呢？
哈利	然後將油槍嘴插入車子的油箱，小心點，管子很重的。好，現在按下加油機上的按鈕，油會開始流出來，把油槍握把上面的板機拉起，就可以加油了。油一加滿，機器會自動停止加油。
菲碧	滿簡單的耶，謝謝！

Pattern Drills

1 At the Full-Service Gas Station 請站務員加油 064

Victor	We're running out of gas. How far is the nearest gas station?
Amy	It's only a few kilometers to the nearest gas station.
	[Five minutes later]
Victor	Fill it up, please.
Attendant	What kind of gas would you like?
Victor	Regular, please.
Attendant	OK.
Victor	How much is that?
Attendant	It comes to $50.

1

My car is out of gas.

Is there a gas station around here?

50 dollars of gas, please.

What is the price per liter?

$3.

2

There isn't any gas in the tank.

Is there a gas station nearby?

3 gallons of gas, please.

How much is it per gallon?

$30.

3

My car is running out of gas.

How far is the nearest gas station?

Fill it up, please.

What does it come to?

$80.

4

Make up your own conversation.

❷ At the Self-Service Gas Station 在自助加油站 🎧065

Phoebe   Excuse me. Can you tell me how to fill up the gas tank?

Harry   Of course. First, run the credit card through the machine, and select the gas you'd like.

Phoebe   What should I do after that?

Harry   Insert the nozzle into the tank of your car. Be careful, the gas hose is very heavy. Now press the button on the pump to allow the gas to flow, and pull the trigger on the handle of the gas hose. The gas will be released into the tank of your car. When the tank is full, the fuel will stop pumping.

Phoebe   Sounds easy! Thank you.

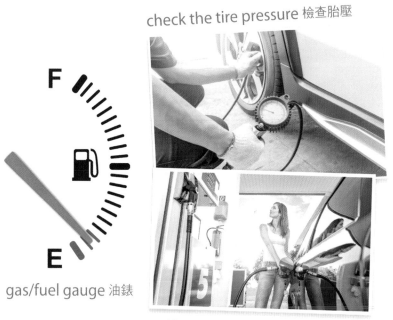

check the tire pressure 檢查胎壓

gas/fuel gauge 油錶

self-service gas station 自助加油站

1 | Could you show me how to fill up the gas tank?

Sure.

How do I use the pump?

2 | Please show me how to use this gas pump.

Certainly.

What do I do next?

3 | Could you tell me how to fill up the gas tank?

Sure thing.

Then what do I do?

4

Make up your own conversation.

At the Hotel:
Checking In

旅館登記住宿

① **reception** 接待櫃檯

② **lobby** 大廳

③ **service bell** 服務鈴

④ **check in** 辦理住宿登記 ⟷ ⑤ **check out** 退房

⑥ **single room** 單人房

⑦ **double room** 雙人房（一張大床）

8 twin room 雙人房（兩張單人床）

9 triple room 三人房

10 suite 套房

11 bath 衛浴設備

12 elevator 電梯

13 key 鑰匙

14 key card 鑰匙卡

⑮ **breakfast** 早餐

⑯ **shuttle bus** 接駁車

⑰ **swimming pool** 游泳池

⑱ **buffet restaurant** 自助餐廳

⑲ **gymnasium (gym)** 健身房

⑳ **sauna** 三溫暖

㉑ **bar** 酒吧

㉒ **tennis court** 網球場

㉓ **coffee shop** 咖啡廳

㉔ **conference room** 會議廳

㉕ **emergency exit** 逃生門

㉖ **bellboy** 大廳服務員
（負責提行李、開房門）

㉗ **doorman** 門房
（負責開關飯店門和計程車門）

㉘ **room maid** 房間打掃人員

㉙ **reservation** 預約

㉚ **vacancy** 空房

㉛ **registration form/card**
登記住宿卡

㉜ **rate** 住宿費

㉝ **deposit** 訂金

㉞ **discount** 折扣

㉟ **tip/gratuity** 小費

㊱ **valuables** 貴重物品

㊲ **wake-up call /
morning call** 晨喚服務

❶ I'd like to check in.
我要辦住宿登記。（已預約住宿）070

Reception	Good afternoon. May I help you?
Steve	Yes. I made a reservation and I'd like to check in.
Reception	Your name, please?
Steve	Steve Johnson.
Reception	Oh, yes. A double room for two nights. Is that correct?
Steve	Yes, it is.
Reception	Would you please fill out this registration card?
Steve	No problem.

接待櫃檯	午安。我能為您效勞嗎？
史提夫	是的。我訂了房間，現在想辦理住宿登記。
接待櫃檯	請問貴姓大名。
史提夫	史提夫‧強森。
接待櫃檯	喔，有。一間雙人房兩晚，對嗎？
史提夫	對。
接待櫃檯	請填寫這張登記卡好嗎？
史提夫	沒問題。

Fill out the registration card
填寫登記表格

❷ Do you have any vacancies now?
請問目前有空房嗎？（臨時住宿）(071)

Sandy	Do you have any vacancies now?
Reception	Certainly, madam. What kind of room would you like to have?
Sandy	A single.
Reception	We have a room commanding a good view of the sea.
Sandy	What's your rate?
Reception	One hundred dollars a night, madam.
Sandy	That's fine. I'll take it.

a room with sea view 海景房

珊蒂	請問目前有空房間嗎？
接待櫃檯	當然，小姐。您想要什麼樣的客房？
珊蒂	單人房。
接待櫃檯	我們有一間可以俯瞰海景的房間。
珊蒂	價錢多少？
接待櫃檯	一天一百元。
珊蒂	好，我要那一間。

1 I'd like to check in.

我要辦住宿登記。(已預約住宿)

Reception	Good afternoon. May I help you?
Steve	Yes. I made a reservation and I'd like to check in.
Reception	Your name, please?
Steve	Steve Johnson.
Reception	Oh, yes. A double room for two nights. Is that correct?
Steve	Yes, it is.
Reception	Would you please fill out this registration card?
Steve	No problem.

1

May I have your name, please?

[Your name]

A triple room for one night.

Yes, I will.

2

Could you spell out your name?

C-H-A-N-G

A suite for three nights.

Certainly.

3

How do you spell your name?

L-E-E

A deluxe guest room for two nights.

Of course.

4

Make up your own conversation.

❷ Do you have any vacancies now?
請問目前有空房嗎？（臨時住宿）🎧073

Sandy	Do you have any vacancies now?
Reception	Certainly, madam. What kind of room would you like to have?
Sandy	A single.
Reception	We have a room commanding a good view of the sea.
Sandy	What's your rate?
Reception	One hundred dollars a night, madam.
Sandy	That's fine. I'll take it.

a vacancy

1

do you need

A double room.

We have a room overlooking the city and with mountain views.

How much is it per night?

2

are you looking for

A room with two beds.

We have a room commanding a view of the surrounding mountains.

How much is a twin room?

3

do you prefer

I'd like to have a room with a single bed.

I can let you have a room with a bath.

What is the rate?

4

Make up your own conversation.

At the Hotel Room

Chapter

11

旅館客房服務

① **air conditioner** 空調

② **light** 電燈

③ **light bulb** 燈泡

④ **safe** 保險箱

⑤ **fridge/minibar** 冰箱；迷你飲料吧台

⑦ **bolt** 門閂

⑥ **lock** 門鎖

⑧ **kettle** 水壺

⑨ **remote control** 遙控器

075

⑩ **hair dryer** 吹風機

⑪ **blanket** 毛毯

⑫ **outlet/socket** 插座

⑬ **towel** 毛巾

⑭ **toilet paper** 衛生紙

⑮ **pillow** 枕頭

⑯ **sheet** 床單

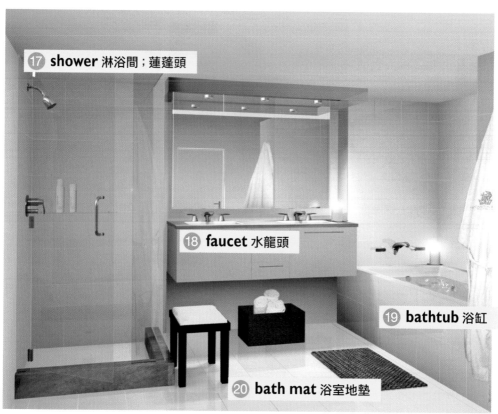

⑰ **shower** 淋浴間；蓮蓬頭

⑱ **faucet** 水龍頭

⑲ **bathtub** 浴缸

⑳ **bath mat** 浴室地墊

㉓ **shampoo** 洗髮精

㉔ **body lotion** 身體乳液

㉒ **soap** 肥皂

㉕ **shower gel** 沐浴精

㉖ **comb** 梳子

㉑ **toilet** 馬桶

㉘ **bath plug** 浴缸塞子

㉗ **Jacuzzi** 按摩浴缸

㉚ **DO NOT DISTURB**
「請勿打擾」告示牌

㉙ **room service** 客房服務

㉛ **PLEASE MAKE UP ROOM NOW**「請打掃房間」告示牌

㉝ **heater** 暖氣

㉜ **alarm clock** 鬧鐘

㉟ **pay movie** 付費電影

㊱ **laundry** 送洗衣物

㊲ **internal call** 內線電話

㊳ **external call** 外線電話

㊴ **long-distance call** 長途電話

㉞ **battery** 電池

㊵ **international call** 國際電話

❶ The . . . in my room doesn't work.

我房間裡的……壞了。 🎧078

Steven	Is this the front desk?
Front Desk	Yes, sir. What can I do for you?
Steven	This is Room 705. The air conditioner in my room doesn't work.
Front Desk	I'll have that taken care of immediately.
Steven	And may I have two more towels, please?
Front Desk	No problem. We'll bring you the towels in just a minute.
Steven	Thanks.

史蒂芬	櫃檯嗎？
櫃檯	是的，先生。請問有什麼需要嗎？
史蒂芬	這裡是 705 號房，我房間的空調壞了。
櫃檯	我馬上派人去處理。
史蒂芬	還有，可以再給我兩條毛巾嗎？
櫃檯	沒問題，我們一會兒就幫您送去。
史蒂芬	謝謝。

❷ A Morning Call 晨喚服務 (079)

Front Desk	Front Desk. What can I do for you?
Angela	This is Room 320. Can I have a morning call tomorrow?
Front Desk	What time do you want us to wake you up?
Angela	Seven, please.
Front Desk	OK. I've set it up for you.
Angela	Thank you.

櫃檯	櫃檯您好，很高興為您服務。
安琪拉	我的房間號碼是 320。明天早上可以叫我起床嗎？
櫃檯	請問您希望幾點起床？
安琪拉	7 點。
櫃檯	好的，已經幫您設定好了。
安琪拉	謝謝。

•Pattern Drills

❶ The . . . in my room doesn't work.
我房間裡的⋯⋯壞了。 🎧080

Steven	Is this the front desk?
Front Desk	Yes, sir. What can I do for you?
Steven	This is Room 705. The air conditioner in my room doesn't work.
Front Desk	I'll have that taken care of immediately.
Steven	And may I have two more towels, please?
Front Desk	No problem. We'll bring you the towels in just a minute.
Steven	Thanks.

hotel maid 房務服務生

housekeeping cart 房務推車

1

How can I help you?

My room number is 706.

The hot water is not hot enough.

May I have an extra blanket?

the blanket

2

May I help you?

This is Room 514.

The light bulb has burned out.

There is no soap in the bathroom. Can you bring me some?

soap

3

Can I help you?

My room number is 1150.

The toilet does not flush.

Do you provide hair dryers?
I need one.

a hair dryer

4

Make up your own conversation.

❷ A Morning Call 晨喚服務

Front Desk	Front Desk. What can I do for you?
Angela	This is Room 320. Can I have a morning call tomorrow?
Front Desk	What time do you want us to wake you up?
Angela	Seven, please.
Front Desk	OK. I've set it up for you.
Angela	Thank you.

當飯店服務人員幫你提行李或送餐點到房間時，你可以先在門邊問「Who is it?」（哪一位？）確認之後再開門。服務人離開時，你應該禮貌性地遞上小費，並說聲「Thank you. (This is for you.)」。

小費約為 1 塊美金或 80 歐分。如果是請服務生送毛巾、毛毯或吹風機之類的東西到房間，則不需給小費。每天早上外出時，也可留下同樣的金額在床頭，給整理房間的服務人員。

1

| May I help you? |
| Room 807 |
| Would you give me a wake-up call? |
| 8:00 |

2

| Can I help you? |
| Room 428 |
| Would you give me a morning call? |
| 7:30 |

3

| How can I help you? |
| Room 1147 |
| I would like to have a wake-up call tomorrow. |
| 6:15 |

4

Make up your own conversation.

In the Restaurant

Chapter

12

在餐廳

① **restaurant** 餐廳

② **waiter** 服務生
waitress 女服務生

③ **menu** 菜單

④ **order** 點餐

⑤ **appetizer** 開胃菜

⑥ **soup** 湯

⑦ **salad** 沙拉

⑧ **main dish /
entrée** 主菜

⑨ **side dish** 附餐

 ⑩ **set meal** 套餐

 ⑪ **specialty /
local food** 當地特產

 ⑫ **dessert** 甜點

 ⑬ **beverage** 飲料

 ⑭ **steak** 牛排

 ⑮ **dressing** 沙拉醬

 ⑯ **spaghetti** 義大利麵

 ⑰ **red wine** 紅酒

 ⑱ **white wine** 白酒

 ⑲ **borsch** 羅宋湯

 ⑳ **Caesar salad**
凱薩沙拉

 ㉑ **seafood** 海鮮

153

22 **beef** 牛肉

23 **pork** 豬肉

24 **lamb** 羊肉

25 **fish fillet** 魚排

26 **shrimp** 蝦子

27 **octopus** 章魚

28 **lobster** 龍蝦

29 **crab** 螃蟹

30 **rib** 肋排

31 **pizza** 披薩

32 **vegetarian dish** 素食

085

33 **spoon** 湯匙

34 **knife** 刀子

35 **fork** 叉子

36 **napkin** 餐巾

37 **grill**
（在烤架上）燒烤

38 **roast**
（用烤箱）烘烤

39 **stew** 燜；燉

40 **boil** 水煮

41 **fry** 油炸

42 **spicy** 辣的
43 **salty** 鹹的
44 **greasy** 油的
45 **tasteless** 沒味道的
46 **raw** 生的
47 **rare** 三分熟的
48 **medium** 五分熟的
49 **medium-well** 七分熟的
50 **well-done** 全熟的
51 **dress code** 服裝規定
52 **check** 帳單

❶ I'd like to reserve a table for two.
我想預訂一張雙人桌。 086

Anthony	I'd like to reserve a table for two, please.
Reception	For what time, sir?
Anthony	Around 8:30 p.m.
Reception	May I have your name please, sir?
Anthony	Yes, Anthony Fox.
Reception	Mr. Fox, we'll hold the table for you for ten minutes. Please be sure to arrive before 8:40.

安東尼	我想訂張雙人桌。
櫃檯	想訂幾點的，先生？
安東尼	晚上 8 點 30 分左右。
櫃檯	請問您貴姓大名？
安東尼	安東尼・福克斯。
櫃檯	福克斯先生，我們會幫您保留座位 10 分鐘，請在 8 點 40 分前到達。

❷ I'll have a steak. 請給我來一份牛排。 🎧087

Waitress	Are you ready to order now, sir?
Jason	Yes, I'll have a steak, please.
Waitress	How would you like the steak: rare, medium, or well-done?
Jason	Rare, please.
Waitress	Would you like something to drink?
Jason	Coffee, please.

服務生	先生，可以點菜了嗎？
傑森	可以，請給我來一客牛排。
服務生	牛排要幾分熟的？是三分熟，五分熟，還是全熟的。
傑森	要三分熟。
服務生	要喝什麼飲料呢？
傑森	咖啡。

❸ How would you like to pay the bill, sir?
先生，您想用什麼方式付帳？ 🎧088

Anthony	Waitress, can I have the bill, please?
Waitress	Yes, sir. How would you like to pay the bill, sir?
Anthony	Do you accept credit cards?
Waitress	Yes, sir. But we only accept American Express, Master card and Visa. What kind do you have?
Anthony	Master card. Here you go.
Waitress	Wait a moment, please.

安東尼	服務生，麻煩買單。
服務生	好的，先生，您想用什麼方式付帳？
安東尼	你們接受刷卡嗎？
服務生	可以，但我們只接受美國運通卡、萬世達卡和威士卡，您用什麼卡？
安東尼	萬世達卡。這裡。
服務生	請稍等。

一般正式的西餐廳，套餐的程序大約是：

| 1. Appetizer 開胃菜 | → | 2. Soup 湯 | → | 3. Salad 沙拉 |

點菜需要花一點時間，如果對菜單有任何不清楚的地方，可以請教服務生。同時，也要注意小費是否已包含在帳單裡。

| 6. Beverages 飲料 | ← | 5. Dessert 甜點 | ← | 4. Main dish (entrée) 主菜 |

如何使用行動支付 How to pay with your mobile phone

① Add your credit card to your payment-enabled mobile phone or device.
在你的手機或行動裝置綁定信用卡。

② Look for the contactless symbol on the terminal at checkout.
在結帳櫃檯尋找感應圖示。

③ Hold your phone or device over the symbol to pay.
將手機或裝置放置於圖示上方感應付款。

註：此種感應支付之手機需支援 NFC 功能，透過 NFC 感應支付的有 Apple Pay、Samsung Pay 與 Android Pay。

❶ I'd like to reserve a table for two.

我想預訂一張雙人桌。 (089)

Anthony   I'd like to reserve a table for two, please.

Reception   For what time, sir?

Anthony   Around 8:30 p.m.

Reception   May I have your name please, sir?

Anthony   Yes, Anthony Fox.

Reception   Mr. Fox, we'll hold the table for you for ten minutes.
            Please be sure to arrive before 8:40.

dress code 服裝規定

1

I'd like to book a table.
madam
At 7:00 tonight.
madam
My name is Norris
Mrs. Norris
7:10

2

I'd like to make a reservation for 5 people this Friday night, please.
ma'am
Around 7:30.
ma'am
Maria Thomas
Ms. Thomas
7:40

3

I would like to reserve a table for tonight.
sir
At 6:45.
sir
Steve Johnson
Mr. Johnson
6:55

4

Make up your own conversation.

❷ I'll have a steak. 請給我來一份牛排。 (090)

Waitress Are you ready to order now, sir?

Jason Yes, I'll have a steak, please.

Waitress How would you like the steak: rare, medium, or well-done?

Jason Rare, please.

Waitress Would you like something to drink?

Jason Coffee, please.

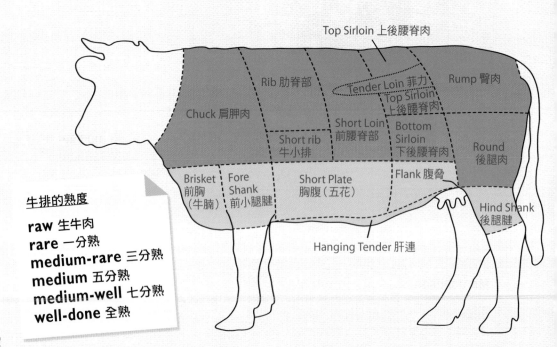

■ Parts Suitable For Broiling and Roasting 適合炙烤和烘烤的部位
▨ Parts Requiring Longer Cooking Methods 需要烹煮較久的部位

Top Sirloin 上後腰脊肉
Rib 肋脊部
Tender Loin 菲力
Rump 臀肉
Chuck 肩胛肉
Top Sirloin 上後腰脊肉
Short Loin 前腰脊部
Bottom Sirloin 下後腰脊肉
Short rib 牛小排
Round 後腿肉
Brisket 前胸 (牛腩)
Fore Shank 前小腿腱
Short Plate 胸腹 (五花)
Flank 腹脅
Hind Shank 後腿腱
Hanging Tender 肝連

牛排的熟度
raw 生牛肉
rare 一分熟
medium-rare 三分熟
medium 五分熟
medium-well 七分熟
well-done 全熟

1

May I take your order now?
Raw
What do you want to drink, tea or coffee?
Tea

2

Are you ready to order?
Medium-rare
What would you like to drink after your meal?
Bring me a cup of Earl Grey tea

3

Would you like to order now?
Medium-well
Would you like coffee, tea, or orange juice?
Orange juice

4

Make up your own conversation.

西餐用餐禮儀
Table Etiquette

1 左叉右刀：

應以左手持叉、右手持刀，將餐巾放在大腿上。

2 刀叉擺放方式：

- 中途若要放下刀叉，應擺放成八字形，代表尚未食用完畢。
- 若是食用完畢，可將刀叉合併擺在一起，則代表已可將餐盤收走。

3 使用順序：

一般來說，會從離餐盤最遠的刀叉開始使用，按每道菜的順序依序使用一種餐具。

4 拿不到遠方的菜餚或調味料時：

若是需要遠方的菜餚或調味料，不應越過他人拿取，可禮貌地向他人詢問，如：「可以遞給我鹽巴嗎？」（**Would you pass the salt, please?**）

不同情況下的餐具擺法
Location of cutlery in different situations

pause 暫停餐點

ready for a second plate
準備好可上下一道菜

excellent 餐點很棒
（已食用完畢）

don't like 不喜歡餐點

finished 已食用完畢

finished 已食用完畢

Fast Food

Chapter

13

速食店

① **hamburger** 漢堡

② **mayonnaise** 美乃滋

③ **pickle** 醃黃瓜

④ **cheese** 起司

⑤ **onion rings** 洋蔥圈　⑥ **chicken nuggets** 雞塊　⑦ **fried chicken** 炸雞

⑨ **apple pie** 蘋果派

⑧ **chicken tender** 雞柳條

(092)

10 **ketchup** 番茄醬　　　**11** **mustard sauce** 芥末醬　　　**12** **barbecue sauce** 烤肉醬

13 **sweet and sour sauce**
糖醋醬　　　**14** **pepper** 胡椒粉　　　**15** **tacos** 墨西哥玉米捲

16 **chicken burger** 雞堡

17 **fish burger** 魚堡

18 **French fries** 薯條

⑲ **hot dog** 熱狗堡

⑳ **bacon** 培根

㉑ **Coke** 可樂

㉒ **iced tea** 冰茶

㉓ **milkshake** 奶昔

㉔ **coffee** 咖啡

㉕ **cream** 奶油

㉖ **sugar** 糖 　　㉗ **hot chocolate** 熱巧克力 　　㉘ **orange juice** 柳橙汁

㉙ **sundae** 聖代 　　㉚ **ice cream** 冰淇淋 　　㉛ **straw** 吸管

㉝ **small** 小的

㉞ **medium** 中的

㉟ **large** 大的

㊱ **refill** 續杯

㊲ **without ice** 去冰

㊳ **flavor** 口味

㊴ **strawberry** 草莓

㊵ **chocolate** 巧克力

㊶ **vanilla** 香草

㉜ **napkin** 餐巾紙

PART 2

·Conversations

❶ Two number 3s, please. 兩份三號餐。 ◠095

Steven	Two number 3s, please.
Clerk	All right. What would you like to drink?
Steven	Diet Coke.
Clerk	Regular or large?
Steven	Regular, please.
Clerk	OK. Anything else?
Steven	No, thanks.
Clerk	For here or to go?
Steven	For here.

hot dog with ketchup 淋番茄醬的熱狗

史蒂芬	我要兩份三號餐。
店員	好的，飲料要喝什麼？
史蒂芬	健怡可樂。
店員	普通杯還是大杯的？
史蒂芬	普通杯。
店員	好的，還要點些什麼嗎？
史蒂芬	沒有了。
店員	內用或外帶？
史蒂芬	內用。

hot dog with ketchup and mustard
淋番茄醬和芥末醬的熱狗

hot dog with ketchup, mustard,
and onions
淋番茄醬和芥末醬、加洋蔥的熱狗

hot dog with ketchup, mustard,
and onions, and relish
淋番茄醬和芥末醬、加洋蔥和佐料的熱狗

❷ What flavor would you prefer? 您要哪種口味？

Clerk	Good afternoon, sir. Can I help you?
Steven	I'd like a hamburger, French fries, and a milk shake, please.
Clerk	What flavor would you prefer, sir?
Steven	I'm not quite sure. What do you have?
Clerk	We have strawberry, chocolate, vanilla, and banana.
Steven	That's fine. I'll try the banana flavor.
Clerk	Anything else, sir?
Steven	No, thanks. That will be all.

店員	午安，先生。您要點什麼？
史蒂芬	我想要一個漢堡、一份薯條和一杯奶昔。
店員	請問您要什麼口味的？
史蒂芬	我也不知道，你們有哪幾種口味？
店員	有草莓、巧克力、香草和香蕉口味。
史蒂芬	好，我要香蕉口味的。
店員	還要什麼嗎？
史蒂芬	不用了，謝謝。這樣就好。

奶昔主要由牛奶和冰淇淋混合而成，以水果口味為多，例如草莓、香蕉、芒果或巧克力等。

•Pattern Drills

1 **Two number 3s, please.** 兩份三號餐。

Steven	Two number 3s, please.
Clerk	All right. What would you like to drink?
Steven	Diet Coke.
Clerk	Regular or large?
Steven	Regular, please.
Clerk	OK. Anything else?
Steven	No, thanks.
Clerk	For here or to go?
Steven	For here.

1

Two happy meals
What is your preferred
Apple juice
No, thanks. That will be all.

2

I'd like a number one
Do you have any preferred
I'd like a small Coke, but don't add too much ice, please
I need some napkins, please.

3

I want a spicy fried chicken meal
What is your choice of
Iced tea
I need some extra ketchup.

4

Make up your own conversation.

❷ What flavor would you prefer? 您要哪種口味？

Clerk	Good afternoon, sir. Can I help you?
Steven	I'd like a hamburger, French fries, and a milk shake, please.
Clerk	What flavor would you prefer, sir?
Steven	I'm not quite sure. What do you have?
Clerk	We have strawberry, chocolate, vanilla, and banana.
Steven	That's fine. I'll try the banana flavor.
Clerk	Anything else, sir?
Steven	No, thanks. That will be all.

對於炸雞部位有特別喜好的人，不妨在點餐時詢問服務生能否更換部位。

chicken breast 雞胸肉

chicken drumstick 雞腿

chicken wing 雞翅

1

| How can I help |
| a hamburger, onion rings, and a sundae |
| hot fudge, hot caramel, and strawberry |
| the hot caramel flavor |

2

| May I help |
| a homemade grilled chicken sandwich, a side salad, and a smoothie |
| blueberry pomegranate, strawberry banana, and mango pineapple |
| the blueberry pomegranate |

3

| May I serve |
| a sausage biscuit, a baked apple pie, and a hot drink |
| hot chocolate, cappuccino, vanilla latte, and brewed coffee |
| the vanilla latte |

4

Make up your own conversation.

Shopping

Chapter
14

購物

Key Terms

1 sunglasses 太陽眼鏡

2 umbrella 雨傘

3 scarf 圍巾

4 glove 手套

5 hat 帽子

6 necktie 領帶

⑦ **swimming suit** 泳衣

⑧ **swimming trunks** 泳褲

PART

❶ **Key Terms**

⑨ **spaghetti-strapped shirt**
細肩帶上衣

⑩ **tank top** 背心

⑪ **T-shirt** T恤

⑫ **long sleeve** 長袖

⑬ **short sleeve** 短袖

⑭ **shirt** 襯衫

⑮ **blouse** 女性上衣

⑯ **sweater** 毛衣

⑰ **turtleneck** 高領上衣

⑱ **suit** 套裝；西裝

⑲ **dress** 洋裝

⑳ **skirt** 裙子

㉑ **jacket** 夾克

㉒ **overcoat** 大衣

㉓ **jeans** 牛仔褲

㉔ **pants** (US) 長褲（美式）
trousers (UK) 長褲（英式）

㉕ **shorts** 短褲

㉖ **sandals** 涼鞋

㉗ **boots** 靴子

㉘ **flip-flops** 人字拖

㉙ **high heels** 高跟鞋

㉚ **leather shoes** 皮鞋

㉛ **sneakers** 運動鞋

㉜ **shoelace** 鞋帶

㉝ **shoe polish** 鞋油

㉞ **socks** 襪子

㉟ **shoulder bag** 側背包　㊱ **handbag** 手提包　㊲ **wallet** 皮夾

㊴ **button** 鈕釦

㊳ **briefcase** 公事包

㊵ **pocket** 口袋

㊶ **cotton** 棉

㊷ **wool** 羊毛

㊸ **silk** 絲

㊹ **leather** 皮革

㊺ **fitting room** 試衣間

㊻ **measure** 測量　　㊿ **fashionable** 時髦的；流行的
㊼ **tight** 緊的
㊽ **loose** 鬆的　　　 51 **old-fashioned** 過時的；老派的
㊾ **fit** 合適；合身

185

❶ May I try on this pair of shoes?

我能試穿這雙鞋嗎？

Yvonne	May I try on this pair of shoes?
Store sales	Of course. What is your size?
Yvonne	I think it's 35.
Store sales	OK. I'll get it for you.
Yvonne	Hmm, they don't feel very comfortable.
Store sales	Try this pair, please. They're made of real leather and are very soft. How do they feel?
Yvonne	They're just right. I'll take them.

怡芳	我可以試穿這雙鞋嗎？
店員	當然可以。您穿幾號？
怡芳	我穿 35 號吧。
店員	好的，我去拿。
怡芳	穿起來不太舒服。
店員	那試試這一款真皮的，比較軟。怎麼樣？
怡芳	這雙很舒服，我就買這雙。

❷ I'd like to buy a shirt. 我想買一件襯衫. (106)

Store sales	May I help you, sir?
Jason	I'd like to buy a shirt.
Store sales	What color do you want?
Jason	I prefer a blue one.
Store sales	What size are you?
Jason	I'm not sure. Could you measure me, please?
Store sales	No problem. I think 40 will be fine for you.
Jason	Can I try it on?
Store sales	Of course. The fitting room is this way, please.

店員	先生您要買什麼嗎？
傑森	我想買一件襯衫。
店員	您要什麼顏色的？
傑森	我要藍色的。
店員	請問您穿幾號？
傑森	我不太確定。你可以幫我量一下嗎？
店員	沒問題。您應該可以穿 40 號。
傑森	我可以試穿嗎？
店員	當然可以，更衣室在這邊。

❶ May I try on this pair of shoes?
我能試穿這雙鞋嗎？ 🎧107

Yvonne | May I try on this pair of shoes?

Store sales | Of course. What is your size?

Yvonne | I think it's 35.

Store sales | OK. I'll get it for you.

Yvonne | Hmm, they don't feel very comfortable.

Store sales | Try this pair, please. They're made of real leather and are very soft. How do they feel?

Yvonne | They're just right. I'll take them.

try on high heel shoes 試穿高跟鞋

clothes shopping 購買衣物

1

Can I try this suit on?
What size?
medium
cotton
very elegant

2

May I try on that pair of high heels?
What size are you?
7
calf leather
the latest fashion

3

May I try that shirt in the window?
What size do you wear?
29
Lycra
chic

4

Make up your own
conversation.

❷ I'd like to buy a shirt. 我想買一件襯衫。 🎧108

zipper 拉鍊

Store sales May I help you, sir?

Jason I'd like to buy a shirt.

Store sales What color do you want?

Jason I prefer a blue one.

Store sales What size are you?

Jason I'm not sure. Could you measure me, please?

Store sales No problem. I think 40 will be fine for you.

Jason Can I try it on?

Store sales Of course. The fitting room is this way, please.

fitting rooms 試衣間

1

I'm looking for a skirt.
What sort of skirt are you interested in?
I'd like to buy a plaid skirt.
L

2

Would you mind showing me some coats?
Do you need an overcoat or a down jacket?
I'm looking for a down jacket.
42

3

I'd like to see some jeans.
Which do you prefer, a light or dark color?
A light color, or even white.
32

4

Make up your own conversation.

Shopping in
the Supermarket

Chapter

15

購物：逛超市

Key Terms 1: Cosmetics

① **perfume** 香水

② **cologne** 古龍水

③ **cosmetics** 化妝品

⑤ **toner** 化妝水

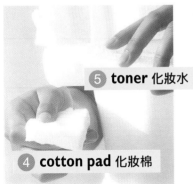

④ **cotton pad** 化妝棉

⑥ **makeup remover /
makeup removing lotion** 卸妝乳

⑧ **pressed powder** 粉餅

⑦ **foundation** 粉底

◢ **BB** cream (blemish balm cream) BB 霜

◢ **CC** cream (color correcting cream) CC 霜

⑨ **puff** 粉撲　　　　　　⑩ **eye shadow** 眼影

⑪ **eye shadow palette** 眼影盤

⑫ **eyebrow pencil** 眉筆

⑬ **eyeliner** 眼線筆

⑭ **mascara** 睫毛膏

⑮ **fake eyelashes** 假睫毛

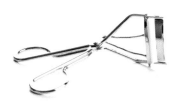

⑯ **lash curler** 睫毛夾

⑰ **lipstick** 口紅

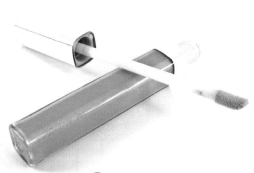

⑱ **lip gloss** 唇蜜

⑲ **lip balm** 護唇膏

⑳ **lip stain/tint** 唇釉

㉑ **blush** 腮紅

㉒ **concealer** 遮瑕膏

㉓ **loose powder** 鬆粉式蜜粉

㉔ **brush** 刷具   ㉕ **lotion** 乳液   ㉖ **cream** 乳霜

㉗ **gel** 凝膠   ㉘ **facial mask** 面膜   ㉙ **mud mask** 泥膜

㉚ **nail polish** 指甲油   ㉛ **nail clippers** 指甲剪

❸❷ moisturizer
保溼用品；潤膚霜

❸❸ essence 精華液

❸❹ oily skin 油性皮膚

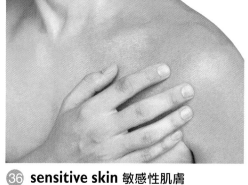

❸❺ dry skin 乾性皮膚

❸❻ sensitive skin 敏感性肌膚

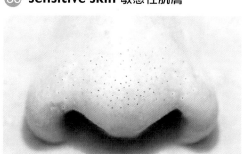

❸❼ acne 粉刺；青春痘

❸❽ blackhead 黑頭粉刺

❸❾ scent 香味

❹❹ base note 後味

❹❹ light 味道淡的

❹❺ floral scent 花香調

❹❹ strong 味道濃的

❹❻ woody scent 木質調

❹❷ top note 前味

❹❼ citrus scent 柑橘調

❹❸ middle note 中味

Key Terms 2: Supermarket

1 **supermarket** 超市

2 **grocery store** 雜貨店

3 **shopping basket** 購物籃

4 **shopping cart** 購物推車

5 **aisle** 走道

Frozen food

6 **frozen food** 冷凍食品

⑦ **deli** 熟食

⑧ **dairy** 乳製品

⑨ **bakery** 烘焙食品

⑩ **beverage** 飲料

⑪ **checkout (counter)** 結帳櫃檯

⑫ **self-checkout** 自助結帳櫃檯

⑬ **express checkout**
快速結帳櫃檯

⑭ **cash-only checkout**
只收現金的結帳通道

⑯ **voucher** 兌換券

⑮ **coupon** 折價券；優惠券

⑰ **potato chips** 洋芋片

⑱ **instant noodles** 泡麵

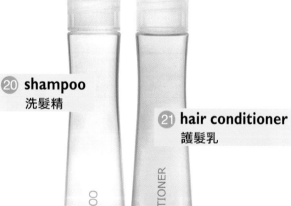

⑳ **shampoo**
洗髮精

㉑ **hair conditioner**
護髮乳

⑲ **chocolate** 巧克力

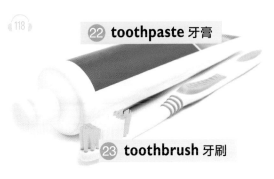

22 **toothpaste** 牙膏

23 **toothbrush** 牙刷

24 **sanitary/maxi pad** 衛生棉

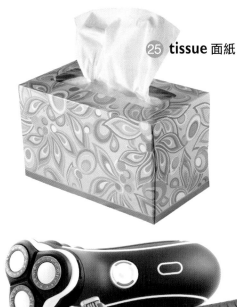

25 **tissue** 面紙

26 **deodorant** 止汗劑

27 **razor** 刮鬍刀

28 **shaving cream** 刮鬍膏

29 **sun protection** 防曬油

30 **mineral water** 礦泉水

31 **juice** 果汁

32 **apple** 蘋果

33 **orange** 柳橙

34 **grape** 葡萄

35 **kiwi fruit** 奇異果

36 **watermelon** 西瓜

37 **pineapple** 鳳梨

38 **banana** 香蕉

39 **strawberry** 草莓

㊵ **lemon** 檸檬

㊶ **cherry** 櫻桃

㊷ **coconut** 椰子

㊸ **melon** 甜瓜

㊹ **peach** 桃子

㊺ **tangerine** 橘子

㊻ **passion fruit** 百香果

㊼ **mango** 芒果

㊽ **pear** 西洋梨

㊾ **avocado** 酪梨

❶ At a Grocery Store 在雜貨店買水果 🎧121

Amy	Excuse me, do you sell apples?
Store sales	Yes. They are over there.
Amy	Do you sell them individually or by weight?
Store sales	By weight. 60 cents per pound.
Amy	Could you weigh these, please?
Store sales	That's $4.55, please. Anything else?
Amy	A bag of cherries, please.
Store sales	Here you are.

a shopping list 購物清單

艾美	請問，你們有賣蘋果嗎？
店員	有，蘋果在那邊。
艾美	是論個賣還是論斤賣？
店員	論斤賣。每磅六十分。
艾美	請秤一下這些好嗎？
店員	四點五十五分。還要什麼嗎？
艾美	請給我一袋櫻桃。
店員	這是你要的櫻桃。

❷ Buying Perfume 買香水 🎧122

Store sales	May I help you?
Amy	Yes. I'm looking for some perfume. Do you have perfumes with a light scent?
Store sales	How about this one? It smells like green tea and is our best seller. Try it.
Amy	It does smell good. How much is it?
Store sales	The price is $40.
Amy	OK. I'll take this one.

店員	有什麼可以為您服務的嗎？
艾美	我想買香水，你們有沒有清淡一點的？
店員	這瓶怎麼樣？它是綠茶的味道，賣得非常好。你可以試用看看。
艾美	真的不錯耶。這瓶多少錢？
店員	40 美金。
艾美	好，那我就買這一瓶。

❸ Buying Lipsticks 買口紅 🎧123

Store sales	May I help you?
Amy	Do you have the latest lipstick from Christian Dior?
Store sales	Yes. What colors do you like?
Amy	Any special colors?
Store sales	How about this one?
Amy	Can I try it on and see how it looks?
Store sales	Of course. This product moisturizes at the same time.
Amy	Looks good. I'll take it.

店員	請問需要什麼？
艾美	你們有賣迪奧最新出的口紅嗎？
店員	有啊，您想要什麼顏色。
艾美	有沒有特別一點的顏色？
店員	這隻好不好？
艾美	我可以試擦看看嗎？
店員	當然可以。這一款口紅的滋潤度很好。
艾美	看起來不錯，就買這隻。

physical storefront;
physical store
實體店面

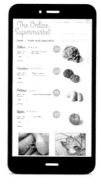

online store
網路店面

❶ At a Grocery Store 在雜貨店買水果 🎧124

Amy	Excuse me, do you sell apples?
Store sales	Yes. They are over there.
Amy	Do you sell them individually or by weight?
Store sales	By weight. 60 cents per pound.
Amy	Could you weigh these, please?
Store sales	That's $4.55, please. Anything else?
Amy	A bag of cherries, please.
Store sales	Here you are.

half a dozen eggs
半打雞蛋

one and a half dozen eggs
一打半雞蛋

18 LARGE EGGS

a dozen eggs 一打雞蛋

1

passion fruit

It is in aisle six.

What else?

A loaf of bread

2

pineapple

It is in the fresh food section

Anything else?

Two bags of corn

3

tangerines

They are next to the food court

Do you need anything else?

Half a dozen eggs

4

Make up your own conversation.

❷ Buying Perfume 買香水 〔125〕

Store sales   May I help you?

Amy   Yes. I'm looking for some perfume. Do you have perfumes with a light scent?

Store sales   How about this one? It smells like green tea and is our best seller. Try it.

Amy   It does smell good. How much is it?

Store sales   The price is $40.

Amy   OK. I'll take this one.

1

| scented candle |
| candles with a floral scent |
| rose |
| $15 |

2

| scented home spray |
| sprays with a woody scent |
| sandalwood |
| $12 |

3

| scented oil for the home |
| fragrance oils with a citrus scent |
| orange |
| $6 |

4

Make up your own conversation.

Prices and Discounts

Chapter

16

殺價與付款

PART 1

Key Terms

 126

① **cash** 現金

② **cash register** 收銀機

③ **credit card** 信用卡

④ **credit card register** 刷卡機

⑤ **cashier** 收銀員

⑥ **bar code** 條碼

⑦ **QR code** QR 圖碼

⑧ **bar code scanner** 條碼掃描器

127

⑨ **discount** 打折

⑩ **price tag** 價格標籤

⑪ **calculator** 計算機

⑫ **cheap** 便宜的

⑬ **expensive** 貴的

⑭ **margin** 利潤

⑮ **receipt** 收據

⑯ **plastic bag** 塑膠袋

⑰ **paper bag** 紙袋

⑱ **gift** 禮物

⑲ **afford** 買得起；付得起
⑳ **reasonable** 合理的；公道的
㉑ **price range** 價格幅度
㉒ **retail price** 零售價

㉓ **reduction** 減少；降低
㉔ **refund** 退款
㉕ **tax** 稅金
㉖ **shipping** 運送

❶ Can you lower the price? 能不能算便宜一點？

Jennifer	Could you show me the T-shirt that's on the model?
Store sales	Here you are. It comes in three different colors: white, blue, and pink.
Jennifer	What's the price?
Store sales	$12.
Jennifer	Can you lower the price?
Store sales	It is already cheap.
Jennifer	I'll take it if you give me a discount.
Store sales	$10. That's the best I can do.
Jennifer	OK. I'll take the blue one.

珍妮佛	我想看一下模特兒身上那件 T 恤。
店員	好的，這是你要看的 T 恤。一共有三種顏色：白色、藍色和粉紅色。
珍妮佛	多少錢？
店員	12 塊美金。
珍妮佛	能不能算便宜一點。
店員	已經很便宜了。
珍妮佛	你幫我打個折我就買。
店員	最低就 10 塊了。
珍妮佛	好吧，那我要藍色的。

❷ How much is that one? 那一個多少錢呢？

Andy	I'm looking for a string of pearls for my wife.
Store sales	Yes, sir. What price range do you have in mind?
Andy	I'm not sure. I don't know very much about the price of pearls.
Store sales	I see. Let me show you some samples of various qualities. This one is very nice. It's three hundred and fifty dollars.
Andy	Is there a price reduction?
Store sales	We are having a sale now. The price has already been reduced.
Andy	How much is that one?
Store sales	It's two hundred and eighty dollars.
Andy	OK. I'll take it. Thank you.

安迪	我想幫我太太買一串珍珠。
店員	好的，先生。您預計購買的價錢是多少？
安迪	還沒決定，是這樣，我不大清楚珍珠的行情。
店員	這樣呀。那麼我給您看一些不同等級的樣品。這串很好看，價格是三百五十美元。
安迪	可以打個折扣嗎？
店員	我們正在大拍賣，價錢已經降低了。
安迪	那條多少錢？
店員	二百八十美元。
安迪	好，我就買這串。謝謝。

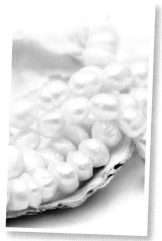

•Pattern Drills

❶ Can you lower the price?
能不能算便宜一點？ (130)

Jennifer	Could you show me the T-shirt that's on the model?
Store sales	Here you are. It comes in three different colors: white, blue, and pink.
Jennifer	What's the price?
Store sales	$12.
Jennifer	Can you lower the price?
Store sales	It is already cheap.
Jennifer	I'll take it if you give me a discount.
Store sales	$10. That's the best I can do.
Jennifer	OK. I'll take the blue one.

國外觀光區的商品定價通常偏高，遊客向老闆殺價或討折扣，幾乎是不可避免的過程。但若是商家已在門口或牆壁貼上 Fixed Price（不二價），表示不願意降價，遊客就不應該再開口殺價，以免顯得不禮貌，成為不受歡迎的奧客。

1

€43

the blouse
How much is it?
€43.
Can you give me a discount if I buy another one?
Can't you lower the price a little?
€40.

2

€58

the sweater
How much did you say it was?
€58.
Are you having a sale today?
Is there a discount for two items?
€100.

3

$176

the dress
What's the price of this item?
$176.
Any discounts?
Could you cut the price a little, please?
$140.

4

Make up your own conversation.

❷ How much is that one? 那一個多少錢呢？ (131)

Andy
I'm looking for a string of pearls for my wife.

Store sales
Yes, sir. What price range do you have in mind?

Andy
I'm not sure. I don't know very much about the price of pearls.

Store sales
I see. Let me show you some samples of various qualities. This one is very nice. It's three hundred and fifty dollars.

Andy
Is there a price reduction?

Store sales
We are having a sale now. The price has already been reduced.

Andy
How much is that one?

Store sales
It's two hundred and eighty dollars.

Andy
OK. I'll take it. Thank you.

1

| a tie |
| my boyfriend |
| ma'am |
| neckties |
| $45 |
| Could you give me a discount? |
| Our prices are already low compared with others. |
| How much does this one cost? |
| $36 |

2

| a pair of diamond earrings |
| my mom |
| madam |
| diamonds |
| $450 |
| Can't you give me a better price? |
| It's the sales price. |
| How much is that pair? |
| $360 |

3

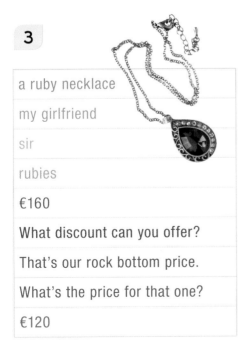

| a ruby necklace |
| my girlfriend |
| sir |
| rubies |
| €160 |
| What discount can you offer? |
| That's our rock bottom price. |
| What's the price for that one? |
| €120 |

4

Make up your own conversation.

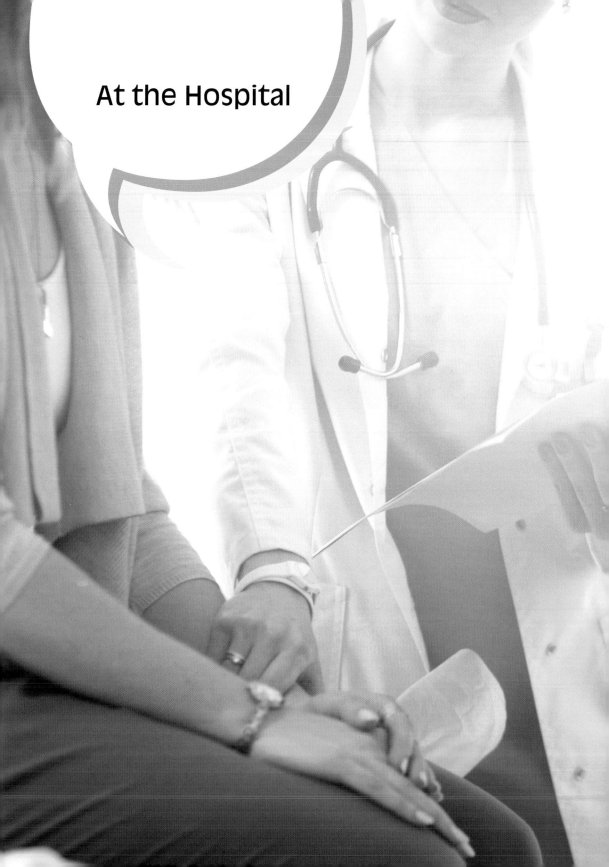

At the Hospital

在醫院或藥房

132

① **ambulance** 救護車

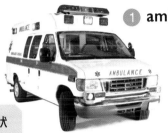

③ **symptom** 症狀

② **doctor** 醫生

④ **sore throat** 喉嚨痛

⑤ **cough** 咳嗽

⑥ **runny nose** 流鼻水

⑦ **sneeze** 打噴嚏

⑧ **stuffy nose** 鼻塞

⑨ **dizzy** 頭暈

⑩ **vomit / throw up** 嘔吐

⑪ **headache** 頭痛

⑫ **stomachache** 胃痛

⑬ **fever** 發燒

⑭ **toothache** 牙齒痛

⑮ **heart attack** 心臟病發作

⑯ **asthma** 氣喘

⑰ **sprain** 扭傷

⑱ **fracture** 骨折

⑲ **allergy** 過敏

⑳ **food poisoning** 食物中毒

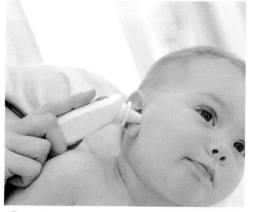

㉑ **take someone's temperature** 量體溫

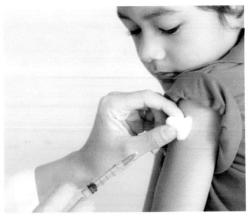

㉒ **take someone's blood pressure** 量血壓

㉓ **injection** 打針

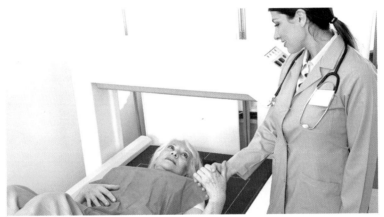

㉔ **check-up** 檢查

㉕ **prescription** 處方箋

(135)

㉖ **pharmacy / drug store** 藥局

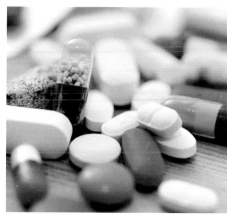

㉗ **medicine** 藥

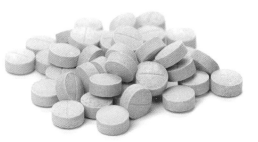

㉙ **pill/tablet** 藥丸

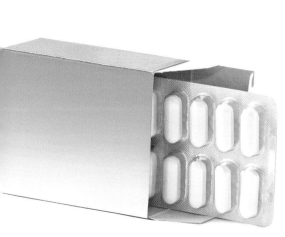

㉘ **painkiller** 止痛藥

㉚ **capsule** 膠囊

③ **powder** 藥粉

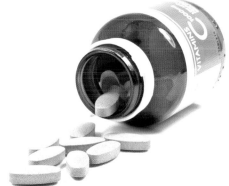

② **vitamin** 維他命

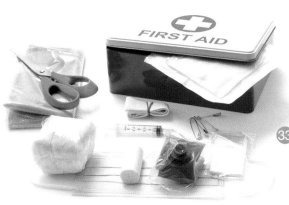

③ **first-aid kit** 急救箱

④ **cotton swab / Q-tip** 棉花棒

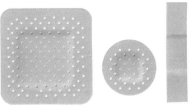

⑤ **Band-Aid** OK 繃（英文採用商標名稱）

137

㊱ **bandage** 繃帶

㊲ **gauze** 紗布

㊳ **eye drops** 眼藥水

㊴ **make an appointment** 預約門診

㊵ **flu** 流行性感冒

㊶ **cold** 感冒

㊷ **jet lag** 時差反應

㊸ **ache** 疼痛

㊹ **bruise** 瘀傷；擦傷

㊺ **cramp** 抽筋；痙攣

㊻ **hiccup/burp** 打嗝

㊼ **fart** 放屁

㊽ **cavity**（牙齒）蛀洞

㊾ **diarrhea** 拉肚子

㊿ **constipation** 便秘

(51) **high blood pressure** 高血壓

(52) **faint** 昏倒

(53) **diabetes** 糖尿病

(54) **insulin** 胰島素

❶ I've got a . . . 我患了……。 🎧138

Peggy	I've got a headache and a sore throat.
Doctor	How long have you had them?
Peggy	Since the day before yesterday.
Doctor	You may have the flu. It's going around now.
Peggy	What should I do?
Doctor	Take some medicine and stay in bed for a day or two.

佩琪	我頭痛，喉嚨痛。
醫生	有多久了？
佩琪	前天開始的。
醫生	我想你是得了流行性感冒，最近正在流行。
佩琪	那該怎麼辦？
醫生	吃些藥，躺著休息一兩天。

Doctor with RX prescription
醫生寫處方箋

capsule 膠囊

❷ At a Drugstore 到藥房買藥 🔊139

Vincent	Have you got anything for diarrhea?
Pharmacist	Yes, here you are. These tablets are very effective.
Vincent	How should I take this medicine?
Pharmacist	Take two tablets every six hours.
Vincent	I see. I'll follow your instructions.
Pharmacist	And rest for a few days.
Vincent	Thank you.

文森	有沒有止瀉的藥？
藥師	有，這是你的藥。這種藥還滿有效的。
文森	這藥該怎麼吃？
藥師	每六小時吃兩顆。
文森	我知道了，我會照指示吃。
藥師	記得休息幾天。
文森	謝謝。

Rx [`ɑr`ɛks]

指醫生開的處方
箋，原符號見左下
圖，出自拉丁字
「recipe」的縮寫

❶ I've got a . . . 我患了……。 🎧140

Peggy	I've got a headache and a sore throat.
Doctor	How long have you had them?
Peggy	Since the day before yesterday.
Doctor	You may have the flu. It's going around now.
Peggy	What should I do?
Doctor	Take some medicine and stay in bed for a day or two.

I have diarrhea. 我拉肚子。

I have constipation.
我便秘了。

allergic reaction to food
對食物產生過敏反應。

1

I have a runny nose.

When did it start?

I've been sick for ten days.

All you need is a few days in bed.

2

I keep coughing.

How many days have you had it?

It started three days ago.

I'll give you a prescription, and you can have it filled at a drugstore.

3

I've had a high temperature for some time now.

Have you had it for a long time?

I've had a bad headache for three days.

Take this prescription to a pharmacy and buy some medicine.

4

Make up your own conversation.

❷ At a Drugstore 到藥房買藥

Vincent   Have you got anything for diarrhea?

Pharmacist   Yes, here you are. These tablets are very effective.

Vincent   How should I take this medicine?

Pharmacist   Take two tablets every six hours.

Vincent   I see. I'll follow your instructions.

Pharmacist   And rest for a few days.

Vincent   Thank you.

x-ray image X光片

blood-pressure meter 血壓計

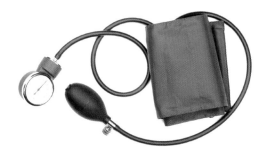

digital thermometer
電子體溫計

stethoscope 聽筒

1

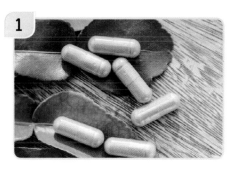

Do you have anything for nausea?
capsules
Take one capsule when you feel like throwing up.
do as you said

2

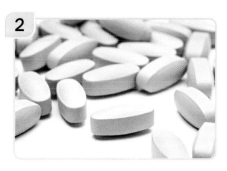

Can you give me something for a cold?
pills
Take one pill every six hours.
do accordingly

3

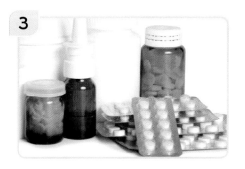

Can I get my prescription filled here?
medicine
Please take it three times a day, after every meal.
do it

4

Make up your own conversation.

彩圖實境

旅遊英語

會話模擬練功

二版

Traveling With English

作　　　者	P. Walsh / Peichien Sun / Feiyueh Chang
編　　　輯	賴祖兒／丁宥榆
主　　　編	丁宥暄
內文排版	劉秋筑
封面設計	林書玉
製程管理	洪巧玲
發 行 人	周均亮
出 版 者	寂天文化事業股份有限公司
電　　　話	+886-(0)2-2365-9739
傳　　　真	+886-(0)2-2365-9835
網　　　址	www.icosmos.com.tw
讀者服務	onlineservice@icosmos.com.tw
出版日期	2021 年 4 月 二版一刷

國家圖書館出版品預行編目 (CIP) 資料

彩圖實境旅遊英語：會話模擬練功
（寂天雲隨身聽 APP 版）/ P. Walsh,
PeiChien Sun, Feiyueh Chang 著
二版 . -- [臺北市]：寂天文化 , 2021.04
　面；　公分

ISBN 978-626-300-001-8　（20K 平裝）

1. 英語 2. 旅遊 3. 會話

805.188　　　　　　　　　　110004617